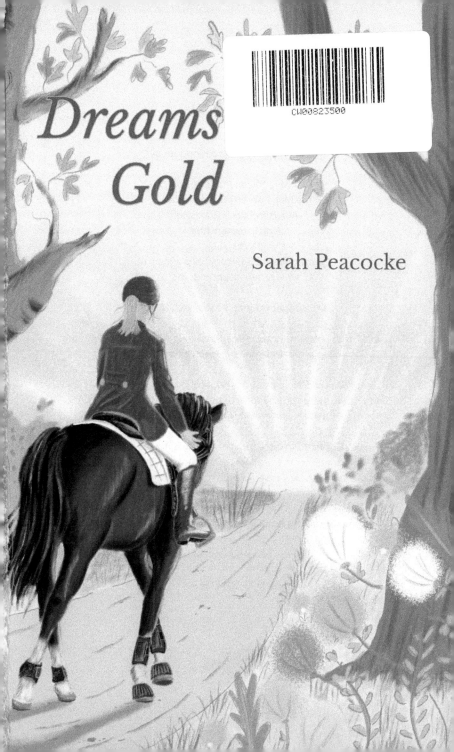

Dreams
Gold

Sarah Peacocke

Published in the United Kingdom by:

Blue Falcon Publishing
The Mill, Pury Hill Business Park,
Alderton Road, Towcester
Northamptonshire
NN12 7LS
Email: books@bluefalconpublishing.co.uk
Web: www.bluefalconpublishing.co.uk

A CIP record of this book is available from the British Library.

First printed August 2021

ISBN 978-1912765447

To my wonderful mother and father,
Beryl and Alex Aitchison,
who made the dreams in this book come true.

And to my two amazing daughters, our showjumping family
across the years, and to friends who've been there to support us
through every high and low...
you know who you are.

Nothing can mean more than to see the British flag raised and
the national anthem played,
whatever sport you enjoy.

Here's to the many dreams we're still waiting to fulfill.

Dreams

of

Gold

Sarah Peacocke

Chapter

1

The Beginning

Georgie woke up to the sound she'd been dreading. A slender branch of the 200 year-old English oak was rhythmically tapping her window while the unmistakable sound of heavy rain pounded against its glass, making her snuggle down even further beneath the duvet that wrapped tightly around her slender 15 year-old body.

Wiping the sleepy dust from the corner of her eyes she struggled to focus on the Thelwell alarm clock she had set to wake her up at 6am. The illuminated hands told her she still had a valuable 10 minutes to wallow in the warmth of her bed before she had to jump out and face the day ahead.

As she lay back, closing her eyes, she began to run through the enormity of the task she faced. She was the only girl in a team of five that had been chosen to compete for her country, Great Britain. And, today, she was leaving with her other team members, crossing the English Channel from Dover to Calais, and driving to

Hagen, a quiet German town some 200kms from the French coast.

She'd dreamt of this moment for as long as she could remember. From the time her mother had put her on her first pony, at the age of five. Star Trek had been a cobby skewbald rescued from the monthly horse market in Reading. When he arrived at their yard he had been thin and scrawny, full of worms, with a rough coat with lice and clumps of matted hair.

His feet had grown long and uneven, forcing his weight onto his heels, his tail touched the ground and his mane fell unevenly on both sides of his neck. Most buyers wouldn't have touched him, but his kind, deep brown eyes had caught her mother's eye, and she'd bid £120 to save him from the certainty of death at one of the many pet food abattoirs.

Star Trek, or Star as he was often called, had done his job well. No-one really knew how old he was, somewhere between 10 and 12, but he proved to be a wonderful first pony, safe and solid, fearless and viceless.

Every weekend her parents would take her, and her sister Vikki, out for rides. They would fight pensioners and cyclists for space on the narrow pavements as they made their way around Cove in Farnborough. The Southampton to Waterloo express would thunder past, but Star wouldn't do so much as blink. The half-way mark would be her grandparents' house, a red brick detached house that backed onto the busy railway line. The tack would come off, Star Trek would get a well-deserved treat of grass from the manicured lawn, and the family would enjoy tea and cake before setting off back home.

As Georgie's confidence grew she started to take control. The leading rein walk around Cove became an outing of the past, to be replaced by trotting and cantering in the rough field next to the Crown and Cushion pub up the road. Rides over the nearby army land followed, and soon a second pony, Black Magic, joined the family.

Magic also came from the market, bought for a similar sum, but he had a glint of naughtiness in his eye, and was always looking for an opportunity to escape, or to take advantage. One day he trod on her father's foot while he was mucking out the stable, and Georgie would swear she had seen him weigh up the situation and, in a planned sort of way, grind his heavy metal shoe onto her father's green welly, leaving him screaming in pain. He limped for quite a few days after that...

The sisters' love of horses had continued into their teens. Ponies had come and gone, mistakes had been made, lessons learned. Pony Club, local shows and gymkhanas had filled the weekends and school holidays. It would be fair to say they were both pony mad, their bedrooms filled with rosettes, their cupboards full of the latest riding wear, and their bookshelves full of horsey tales.

As their experience grew, the need for better, more experienced ponies grew too. Vikki fell in love with a 4 year-old 14.2 dun, barely broken, called Nugget, found on a local farm. She was determined she would ride him, and for several weeks things went well. Then, as they rode out into the woods one day, Nugget took fright, reared, spun round, unceremoniously dumped Vikki face first onto a tar road, and galloped home.

Vikki was rushed to hospital, needing stitches on her nose and upper lip, and while the wounds healed, the scars didn't. She never stopped riding, but somehow some of the confidence was gone. Nugget was sold, and in his place came Dolly, a wonderful chestnut mare who, over the months ahead, gave Vikki back her confidence and a desire to compete.

The sisters' first serious pony was a palomino, bought through an advert in Horse and Hound, and tried at a yard in Petersfield. Vishtaspa, or Tasper as he quickly became known, broke all the rules. Although he wore a running martingale, his head was always held up high, as though he knew of his pride and, as he cantered towards a fence, it would rise even higher. They gave up wondering how he could see what was in front of him, as he would clear fences with ease.

One day, at the local hunter trials at Wellington Country Park, Georgie pleaded for the chance to compete Tasper in the bigger class. Against her better judgement, but faced with continual pleading, her mother gave in. The fear she felt as her slight 11 year-old handled the 14.2 pony around the solid course of 3ft 3ins fences was immense. Never had she been so pleased to see the pair gallop through the finish, clocking up a fast time with just five penalties for a run out in a little copse out on the course.

Georgie could still remember that day, as clearly as anything. In her mind's eye she could go over every fence and remember every line. As she lay in bed that wet and cold spring morning she realized it had been the start of her desire to win. From deep inside her being, she recognised the thrill of competing, and the satisfaction of taking home a rosette, especially a red one. That day changed the course of her life forever.

Chapter

2

Getting Ready

The door creaked open slightly and her mother switched on the light.

"Come on Georgie, wake up, there's still so much to do, and the box will be here in a little over an hours' time. We must be ready."

Georgie sat up and took a gulp from the glass next to her bed. Running to the bathroom she cleaned her teeth, then brushed her hair, pulling it back tightly from her face and putting it into a ponytail. The shower would come later once her pony had left.

Pulling on a T shirt, jumper and leggings, she ran down the stairs, snatching a piece of toast spread with her favourite marmite, before pulling on her boots and thrusting her arms into her jacket.

Letting the kitchen door slam in the wind, she ran round to the yard, where the lights were already blazing, and her groom Lizzie was beginning the morning ritual of feeding and mucking out.

Five inquisitive heads turned to see her run onto the

yard, several nickering quietly, giving her a welcome she loved to hear. She went to each in turn, pulling a polo from her jacket pocket, placing it on the palm of her hand, and loving the gentle touch of their lips as they sucked the peppermint from her skin.

First there was Tina, a stunning grey mare bought from Ireland, with the rather grand registered name My Lady Blue. Tina was her favourite, she'd carried her to many firsts, most notably taking her to a clear round in the massive Paul Fabrications series at South View that January. She could still remember the thrill of getting through the finish without faults and being one of just four clear rounds.

"We're off on a very special journey today," she whispered in her ear. "You can't come with us this time, but you will next, I promise."

Moving to the next box she was amused to see Azzie, a rotund skewbald mare, trying to reach out for her pocket before she could get to the polo. "Hold on a minute, you greedy mare, let me get your treat out," she said.

Azzie, registered as Just Two Tone because of her striking brown and white patches, was the first novice she had produced. Bought with just a few pounds on her record, Georgie had patiently worked with this hot-headed mare, qualifying her for the Junior Newcomers Second Rounds, and was convinced she had a chance of making the Horse of the Year Show final with her later that year.

"It isn't your turn this time either," she said. "But be good, enjoy a peaceful weekend in the field. When we get back, there's going to be plenty of work for you to do."

Tasper was already calling out to her from the third box impatiently kicking the stable door with his foot, knowing the polo was coming. "Quiet boy, it's coming," she said, gently rubbing his muzzle as he grabbed the mint. Not for the first time she thought about the number of polos that must be fed to horses and ponies, rather than humans.

Moving on to the fourth of the wooden boxes, at the same time savouring the smell of the fresh shavings that had been liberally spread in each stable, the early morning mucking out nearly completed, she reached up to pat the chestnut head of her very first horse, Katy.

By the famous show jumping stallion, Clover Hill, Katy's Clover was a 15.2 five-year-old mare that was just the right size to introduce her, early, to the horse ranks. Riding the novice classes, she was learning the difference in length of stride and preparing for the year when she was 16 and would leave the pony ranks to become a junior rider, sometimes competing against people twice or even three times her age and experience.

Although still young in experience, Katy was the perfect teacher. She loved her job, would gallop faultlessly around senior classes as long as the fences weren't too high, and was the perfect angel to look after. If Azzie was the punk rocker of the yard, Katy was the aristocratic country lady.

As she moved on to the fifth box she could sense this stable was the centre of attention. The occupants' head was already missing from the half open door, with this talented mare already tethered to the ring at the back of her stable. Her rugs off, piled safely in the corner, she was pawing the ground impatiently while waiting for the grooming that would make her coat gleam like a mirror.

Opening the door quietly, Georgie walked in. This bay mare, as slight as a racehorse but as powerful as a jet engine, was the pony her country had come to rely on.

Allie had been in her yard just seven months. Getting her name from a nickname linked to the month of April in which she was born, she'd arrived with an enviable record. She had European gold medals and just about every major championship to her name. When she'd come up for sale the price tag was enormous, higher than that of the latest Mercedes Sports car, and certainly a world record price for a show jumping pony.

She was believed to be the product of an accidental mating, between a thoroughbred stallion and an ordinary mare, somewhere near a village in

Staffordshire. From there her first owners had chosen her name, April Days.

Walking towards her, Georgie smiled as the mare flattered her ears to her head. She wasn't one for a cuddle or a hug. She was a professional machine. She knew her job inside out, and somehow sensed this was the start of an important journey.

"Grab the bandages and start with her tail," said Lizzie. 'Don't do it too tight because it will be on for a long time, we'll put a tail guard on top. We don't want her to rub her tail in the box."

Georgie dampened the bandage slightly in a nearby bucket and moved behind her, talking quietly as she went. Picking up her tail she delicately wound the bandage from the top, taking care to tie it securely.

Her mane was short and even, ready to plait on the days of competition. Running her fingers through it, Georgie was amazed by its softness. Picking up a body brush she put one hand on her headcollar, using the other with rhythmic strokes to remove every bit of dust from her intelligent head. Allie's eyes gazed into Georgie's, both halves of this partnership understanding the importance of the job ahead.

"This is it Allie, the weekend I've waited so long for," Georgie whispered. "We're in this together, we're a team, and we're going to win. We can't let one another down. This is so important."

Allie shook her head, as if in acknowledgement of

the expectation. Georgie smiled, patted her gently, and went to the tack room to fetch her bandages, dodging the heavy drops of rain as she ran. Running back, she went back into the stable and pulled the lead rope free, moving Allie outside her box, under the cover of the overhang. First, she set about applying the dark black hoof oil, spilling it out into a bowl then painting it carefully onto the bottom of each hoof just as she would apply nail varnish to her own fingernails.

As she waited patiently for it to dry, she went back to the tack room to see what Lizzie was doing. Running through a checklist, her groom was putting every item of tack to one side, checking it as she went, and making certain nothing was left behind.

First there was the Pessoa close contact saddle, black, with suede knee rolls to help to keep her leg tight against Allie's body. The stirrup leathers were run up the saddle, holding safety stirrups with rubbers, designed to give extra grip and slip off the foot easily in the event of a fall. The wide matching girth, elasticated at either end, would allow the mare to stretch over a fence without fear.

The black Whitaker bridle gleamed, the soft snaffle bit and drop noseband gentle but offering control, with a headpiece that jingled as it was moved, holding two precious lucky charms that had stayed with the mare as she changed homes over the years. The running martingale was already attached to the bridle, the rubber reins offering extra grip in the event of rain.

A selection of rugs was folded neatly. Top of the pile was a white sweat rug, looking like a giant string vest, its holes allowing for ventilation but, at the same time, capturing warmth after a competition round. A thick stable rug in case it turned cold, then an under blanket, again a precaution in case the weather changed. A thin rain sheet was over the top, looking outside it seemed this was going to be a key part of the packing.

Two filled hay nets for the journey were waiting in the yard, along with a selection of buckets and two bags of carefully mixed feed provided by one of her sponsors, Spillers. The high energy mix and nuts gave Allie just the right amount of fizz without the pop.

Leaving Lizzie to finish her tasks in peace, Georgie went back inside to the farmhouse kitchen, sitting down to a bowl of cereal while talking about the excitement of the weekend to her father.

"I wish you were coming to watch us Dad," she said. "I know there's a lot to do here, but this is such a special weekend. It's the first time I've ridden abroad on a British team, and I have to go well to stand a chance of being selected for the Europeans."

Joe nodded knowingly. "I know darling, but someone has to look after the ponies you're leaving behind. Like it or not, they can't look after themselves. Then there's the chicken, the cats and the dogs, not to mention the fieldwork and garden. Don't worry, I'm going to be very busy while you're gone, and I'll be in touch all the time on the phone."

Finishing her breakfast, with her phone telling her the lorry was running 15 minutes late, she ran upstairs for a quick shower before it arrived. Her clothes were already packed, her show jacket, now proudly carrying the British flag on one lapel, and three pairs of jodhpurs safely packed inside a protective cover, ready to load into the wardrobe of the lorry. Her father had polished her long leather boots the night before, managing a shine that even a private in the army would be proud of producing.

Her brown leather suitcase, holding her neatly folded show shirts as well as her casual clothes, was so full she had to sit on it to make it shut. Now it was ready to take downstairs and put in the car her mother would drive behind the horse box.

Georgie was lucky that her early successes had attracted several sponsors, each helping with the running costs of her team. Spillers provided the horse feed, Horseware the rugs and outdoor clothing, Sarm Hippique a lot of her showring clothing and a catalogue company her tack and grooming kit.

As she sat on her bed, running through everything in her mind, she heard the unmistakable hiss of air brakes as the modern Oakley horsebox reversed into her drive. Her ponies, sensing some new arrivals, whinnied loudly across the yard, their calls of greeting returned from inside the lorry where the other four ponies were already safely standing.

"Georgie, they're here," called her mother up the stairs. "Let's move."

Georgie bounded down the stairs and ran out into the drive. Mark, the father of one of the other selected riders, was walking round to the back of the horsebox to let down the ramp. Allie was the last of the ponies to be loaded.

Lizzie led her round from the stable block, and you could see her eyes light up with excitement when she saw the waiting lorry. She nickered to the ponies already on board and ran up the length of the ramp, eager to start her journey. "She certainly knows she's off on a trip," said Georgie, "it always surprises me how easy she is to travel. She's so intelligent."

It didn't take long to store the tack, feed and clothes into the box, tie up the haynets, push up the ramp, and pull out of the drive. Next stop Dover, where all the paperwork would be checked, and the lorry would catch one of the many P&O crossings to Calais. Hurriedly putting her suitcase into the waiting Saab, she shouted a rushed goodbye to her sister, who hugged her for luck, and got into the front seat, quickly buckling up her belt.

"I'm going to come back with a medal and a rug," she shouted to her father over the noise of the engine. "We're going to win."

Chapter
3

Looking Back

The journey to Dover took nearly three hours. They skirted around Guildford on the A3 before joining the M25, getting stuck in roadworks near the Gatwick turn off before the road cleared and they had a straight run to the historic port, famous for its towering white cliffs.

As they sat silently in the car, Georgie sat back and remembered how Allie had come into her life the previous November.

The pony already had an awesome reputation. She had been to three European championships, and won five gold medals. She had started her life with an inexperienced girl in Staffordshire, her uncanny ability to jump propelling her into the limelight. The mare had been sold from there and moved across the Irish Sea to a home near Belfast for the following two years.

All riders stay on ponies until the year of their 16th birthday then, like it or not, if they want to stay in the show jumping world, they have to move on to horses. So, that autumn, Allie had come on to the market. Her teenage rider was distraught and had pleaded with her parents to let her keep her, but everyone knew this mare had such a desire to jump, that to turn her out into a field would destroy her soul.

Gone were the days when a pony could be taken into the horse ranks. The famous Stroller with Marion Coakes had stood a little over 15hh and managed the senior courses in the 1970s, but now the tracks were more difficult and the distances longer. They were no place for a pony, no matter how talented.

Georgie's mother had heard about Allie, she had built an awesome reputation, but had never seen her jump. Not even on video. Her talent was enormous, but so was her price tag.

That October her mother had been approached to see whether she was interested in the pony. She was being marketed quietly, behind the scenes. Selectors had been watching Georgie and spotted her potential and felt she might be the right partner for this unusual mare.

Jane had sat down with her daughter and had a long and very serious talk. Did she want to ride the mare? If so, she must promise that, should she be bought, she would never complain, would learn to ride the mare however difficult she was, and get back on, no matter how many times she fell off. Georgie agreed to all these terms and started to pray each night that this magic pony would come to her yard.

Just over a year before, her grandmother had died. She'd lived a careful and quiet life, and Georgie had really fond memories of her holidays with her on the Isle of Wight. Of coloured sands at Alum Bay, funfair rides and trampolines in Ryde, watching the street carnivals and throwing money up on to the passing floats in Sandown and Shanklin, and playing croquet on the lawn at her grandparent's home in Playstreet Lane.

Her grandfather, Alex, had wanted to do something special with the money his wife, Beryl, had saved. He was missing his wife terribly, and Georgie's mum knew that if she bought the pony, it would give him a new lease of life. He would be able to follow his granddaughter's career, travel with her to shows, and proudly stand next to her when and if she won awards.

The deal was done, the pony changing hands for a record sum, the price of a small house or apartment and, once a full vetting was completed, the travel arrangements were made.

Concerned about the money outlaid, a special horse box was commissioned to bring her across the Irish sea on her own... the risk of her travelling with other horses where she could be jostled and injured was just too great.

Georgie had been jumping her other ponies at West Wilts Equestrian Centre when her father had rung. "She's arrived, she's in her stable," he said. "But goodness knows what all the fuss is about, she's tiny. There's nothing of her under the rugs."

She couldn't wait to get home that evening and, as soon as the lorry pulled to a halt in the yard, was out of the lorry door, running round to the specially prepared box that would house this equine star. As soon as she walked into the stable, Georgie saw what her father had meant. Her immediate reaction was the same. One of surprise, and almost horror. The pony she had heard so much about resembled a miniature racehorse.

She was bay in colour, with a small white blaze on her head. Her legs were fine, her coat so thin Georgie wondered how she could keep her warm without layers of rugs, her eyes deep brown and kind, her mane and tail neat and straight. She could barely hide her disappointment but knew better than to say anything.

"Let's let her settle, we'll put her out for some exercise in the ménage tomorrow," she said, almost dismissively. Offering her a polo, she was amazed when the mare sniffed the peppermint and then turned away, almost in disdain.

The ponies she'd competed at West Wilts were unloaded from the box, their travelling bandages and rugs removed, and feed and water given as they were settled for the night, Georgie watched their reaction to the new arrival. They sniffed, snorted, squealed, and nipped at one another across the open stable divides.

Gradually, as they settled, she turned off the lights, and went indoors.

Tomorrow was another day. Maybe she would get on the mare and see what all the fuss was really about.

That night she dreamed about winning the European championships. It had been her ambition for as long as she could remember. Now she knew she had the opportunity but understood the reality was still a long way off.

The next day she was up early, keen to see how Allie had settled. In the daylight the mare still looked as ordinary as she had the night before. An hour after watching her polish off her breakfast, seeing that there was nothing wrong with her appetite, she took her bridle from the tack room wall and walked back to her box.

Too frightened to use a headcollar, just in case she took fright on the way to the ménage, she put the bit in the palm of her hand noticing how her head came down to her hand, willingly accepting the sweet iron roller.

Tucking the headpiece behind her ears, she did up the throat lash and talked soothingly to her as she put the reins over her head and led her across the concrete to the open gate of the ménage. She noticed how Allie sized everything up. She sensed immediately the mare had intelligence she had never seen before.

Once inside the school she shut the gate and slipped

off the bridle. Expecting the mare to go mad, to buck, kick, squeal and gallop, as she was set free for the first time in a week, she stood clear. Yet again she was surprised. Allie walked around all four sides of the arena, sniffed at the wooden rails, bent through them to grab some blades of luscious grass, then stood silently in the middle, as though sizing up her new home. A few minutes later, clearly content with her environment, she walked back to Georgie, gently nuzzling her.

The temptation to ride her was immense, but Georgie knew she had endured a long journey and must be tired. She was determined to give her at least a day to settle in. Yet Allie seemed to want to be ridden, her eyes almost pleading, taking in the pile of jumps stored at the far end of the school.

"OK girl you win. Let's do some work then," she said, taking her back to the yard to saddle her up, and put on the overreach boots that would protect her heels, and the tendon boots that would stop her from knocking her legs. "We'll see how you feel."

Gently easing herself into the saddle, she was surprised at how short and low the mare's neck was. Even at a walk she could sense she had nothing in front of her. If Allie were to mess about, and put down her head, Georgie couldn't imagine how she would manage to stay on. As they walked around the ménage together, on a loose rain, they were trying each other out - much as you would test drive a car – looking for weaknesses, trying out basic commands, and seeing how comfortable they felt together.

Later Georgie was to remember this first ride well. She hated it. Positively hated it. The mare did nothing wrong, but Georgie sensed nothing unusual. None of the magic she had expected. Instead, she felt as though she was sitting on a razor blade, and worse still, knew she had nothing in front that would help her balance. For the second time she was horrified. And she knew she could still say nothing – she had promised to master this mare, whatever this was going to take.

As she rode her other ponies, some of her confidence came back. Surely the mare had to have something special about her to have been so successful – or had the riders been so good, they had made this mare into what she had become? Even at this point she was already somewhat of a legend in her lifetime.

Going back into the house for some lunch, she decided to look at the fancy folder that had arrived with the pony.

As well as the usual FEI passport and some pictures of her jumping with her previous owner, to her horror there was a long sheet of lined paper that detailed everything that should, and shouldn't be done, with the pony.

Top of the list was the fact that the fencing in any field she was put into had to be at least 6ft 6ins high, or Allie would jump out. Filled with concern she rushed outside to ask her father how high the post and rail in her paddocks measured. "Oh, I'd say between 4ft 6 and 5ft," he replied. Very quickly he learnt he was going to get his work cut out to heighten the fence as a priority.

Next up was a list of how she should be fed and how much exercise she should have every day.

Georgie had never received such detailed instructions before and was a little confused as to how much attention she should give them. She decided to wait until the morning to discuss the right management methods with her trainer, and carefully put the folder to one side.

William was coming the next day, to give her a first lesson. Maybe once he was there, the secret to her management and success would be unlocked.

The following day she was already riding Allie when Will's car pulled into the driver. "Hi Georgie, how does she feel?" he asked. "Ordinary," she replied. "Very ordinary."

"Right, lets warm up a bit more and then pop a couple of decent cross poles," he said, asking Lizzie to help him move some of the heavy BSJA jumps into the centre of the arena. Carefully walking out the right distance, he put up a grid of ground poles followed by a small cross.

"Come in on the right rein in a nice working trot,"

he said. "She knows exactly what she's doing, so try to leave her head alone."

Georgie did as she was told and could immediately sense the mare pick up as she saw the distant jump. Down the line she went, but to her surprise the pony hit the cross pole hard, knocking it to the ground. Her heart sunk even deeper. If Allie couldn't pop a fence 70 cms in height, how on earth could she jump a course at 1.40m?

"Don't worry about that," said Will, sensing her concern. "This mare won't start to operate until we get to a decent height. I just want you to get used to her feel."

Several more times she came down the same line, alternating her approach rein. Each time the mare popped the fence, but each time she rubbed it, doing nothing to fill her rider with confidence.

"OK, let's start to see what we have here," said Will, "walk her around a little while Lizzie and I put up a few fences." All the time her parents had been quietly watching from the bedroom window – they too were getting more concerned by the moment.

"Gosh, what on earth have I bought?" asked her mother Jane. "This is going to be the most costly mistake in my life. She looks so ordinary."

Will carried on making his course of five jumps, making each a little larger than the last. The final fence was a set of planks, the one obstacle that had always been a bit of a bogey for Georgie. Her heart sunk when she saw what he had built.

"Right, a nice working canter, and keep the rhythm all the way round," he said, telling her the route to take. As she approached the first fence, she was full of trepidation. But the mare took over, pulling her towards the simple upright, gauging the take-off distance and popped over the-metre-high fence, promptly bucking as she landed the other side. "Sit back," shouted Will. "Gather her up before you approach the second."

Coming to the second she could sense the enthusiasm in the mare beneath her. She suddenly felt so different. She knew what she was doing, her ears were pricked, her head set, and nothing was going to stop her jump.

Each time she landed she bucked, and each time Georgie realized how hard she was going to have to work to stay on. She felt clumsy and unbalanced, alarmed at how she was riding, but at least the mare was jumping.

The planks were set at an angle off the top corner. As she approached them, by far the largest fence on the track, she could feel her stomach churn. But Allie had no reservations. Tucking herself up she soared over the top, giving them inches of air. At that moment Georgie felt what it was like to fly – and her parents, still watching, turned and gave one another a hug. This was what it was all about.

Will realized Georgie was still not convinced. She was talking to him about her love for her grey mare Tina, who the previous week had jumped clear in the Paul Fabs qualifier at South View. She was convinced she was the better of the two.

He quietly went about his work – he was a man of few words – and built three of the fences higher. The planks he set at the maximum pony height, 1.30m. They looked huge, especially on a new pony she had only sat on twice.

Allie continued her bucking display, and it was all Georgie could do to stay in the saddle. As she turned to the last, the formidable planks, she could sense a difference in the mare. Playtime was over. She came to the planks, measured the distance, and soared over them clearing the top of the wings. There was no buck the other side.

"Wow, that felt amazing," she said. "I've never had that feeling that over a fence."

Will smiled to himself. He'd seen enough. This mare met every expectation he had. He was going to be training a European championship winner. He didn't need to see any more.

Georgie took some more convincing over the weeks ahead, but gradually she came to trust Allie, and understood how intelligent she was. For the first three months the bucking continued, both inside and outside the ring – it was as though Allie was teaching her how to ride her properly. Then, as suddenly as it had started, it stopped, and Georgie knew in her heart their partnership was cemented. They were one.

Chapter
4

Building the Partnership

There were two things her parents hadn't really considered when they bought Allie. One was the jealousy of other riders and parents, many of whom they had come to consider as friends. The other was the enormous pressure they were putting on their daughter, riding a pony with an international reputation while she hadn't come up through the more 'normal' top equestrian family.

Watching the show groom unloading the ponies one by one and getting each checked by the Dover vet so all the temporary export paperwork was correct, Georgie was remembering the first time she took Allie to a show.

Under the cover of darkness, they'd entered an unaffiliated show jumping competition at Priory Equestrian, a local show centre well known for grass routes classes. They entered the clear round only, using Allie's unregistered name so no-one picked up who she was, and after a good warm up in the cold outside warm up area, entered the ring to the announcer reading out Georgie's name.

Georgie could remember how nervous she was. She had only jumped the mare at home and had no idea how she would perform in the ring. Some horses are perfect at home and then behave really badly at shows, others show nothing at home and then jump their socks off in the ring.

So far Allie had behaved impeccably, bucking after the practice fence, but feeling effortless as she popped the upright and then the oxer.

As the bell rang Georgie went over the course again in her head. It was so easy to forget your way around a course with up to 14 different jumps to remember. Even at this level it was a challenge.

The first half of the course went well, and Georgie could feel her pony enjoying her round, but also sensed her questions – why are we jumping so low – where's the audience – where are the cheers?

Coming to a dog-leg Georgie lost her concentration for a second and realised she was half a stride off the fence. As she pushed to make up the extra distance, she heard the all-to-familiar clang as the top rail fell to the floor. As she went through the finish she heard the words 'four faults' from the announcer.

She was gutted. Her first competition on this elite mare and she had failed her in a simple clear round competition. No rosette to take home, and at this point any thought of the European Championships seemed impossibly far away.

She soon cheered up once home and relating the story to her dad, who as usual had stayed at home to look after the rest of the household menagerie.

Next up she remembered their first affiliated competition, a competition run under British Showjumping rules. They'd travelled down to Hand Equestrian Centre near Bristol and entered the open competition for registered JA (the highest level) ponies the day before New Year's Eve.

This was to be the first time anyone had seen her ride Allie and, as word spread, lots of people had travelled to the venue, some of them, sadly, hoping for a disaster.

All went well in the collecting ring and, as she waited in the shute to be let into the ring, her stomach was full of butterflies. She knew so many eyes were on her, including those of the Chairman of the British Showjumping, whose son was competing against her and who would be one of the selectors looking for future team members.

Saluting to the judges box she heard the bell ring and cantered to the first. Maintaining a steady rhythm in an arena where you could hear a pin drop, she jumped her first clear round of so many to come. Muted applause welcomed her as she left the ring and went to study the course for the jump off.

Hugging her mum she said: "I can't believe it. My first open, at my first affiliated show, and I've jumped clear. Allie took me round Mum, she felt so good and so keen to show everyone how it's done." There were smiles all round and lots of polos for Allie, who by now had fallen in love with these peppermint snacks.

At the end of the first round there were eleven combinations to go against the clock, and Georgie was drawn 7th. She knew she wasn't really ready to push for a win, still not certain how tight she could turn her mount up, but she was determined to jump clear and put in a good performance.

When the time came her competitive spirit took over and she decided to have a go. Galloping to the last she knew she had done enough to get a good place, but not to win. Jumping double clear she was handed her first rosette for this new partnership, a blue one signifying second place, beaten by a tiny margin by the son of her watching selector.

Georgie didn't remember much more about that day. But she remembered she had proved a lot of people wrong that day, people who said she would never be able to ride Allie, and people who wanted her to fail. Yes, she was an expensive pony, but in Georgie's view then, worth every penny, and no, she wasn't easy to ride. But she had stuck to the promise she made to her mum and over the past three months had begun to master how to ride this superstar.

Chapter
5

Hagen

As they approached Dover, Georgie pulled her thoughts back to the present, and the challenge that lay ahead. There were five ponies and five riders making up this British Nations Cup squad, all carefully selected by the Chef d'Equipe and BS selection team, on their results so far this year.

Although they were still a couple of months from the selection of the team that would contest the Europeans, Georgie knew this was a trial, especially for her. Her pony had the experience, but she didn't. And while the boys travelling with her were riding ponies not so successful, they came from thoroughbred backgrounds and never seemed to expose a nerve.

First there was Robbie. He was the oldest son of Britain's most formidable show jumping star. He was a year younger than Georgie, but had been competing professionally all his life, in 128s, 138s and now 148s. He was the playboy of the team, always chatting up the girls, and leading the others into trouble.

Georgie could never understand why the girls fell for him, even her best friend had gone out with him for a while. She supposed it was because of who he was, rather than what he was. He had quite a quick temper on him then, something Georgie didn't like to see.

More than once she had seen him jump off and throw the reins at a waiting groom when it hadn't gone his way in a final, storming into his box, kicking the ground or throwing something like his whip on the ground or at the side of the lorry.

But she knew Robbie had many advantages, not least his parents' support, and also access to some of the best ponies in the world, simply because of his name. At this point she was certain she could compete on equal terms and had got the better of him in many recent competitions.

Next there was Robbie's best friend, Davey. He was also the son of a show jumping star. His father owned a well-known equestrian complex in Wales, and although Georgie sensed he didn't always see his future in this equestrian sport, certainly not at the same dizzy heights enjoyed by his father, at the moment he was following in the hoofprints of the family business.

Davey would always tease her. She remember how the last Christmas she'd got a card from him, professing his undying love, and saying he planned to marry her in the future. Smiling to herself, she remembered that sentiment had lasted just a few brief hours, until the next blonde, adoring, fan had come along.

Robbie and Davey together were a nightmare, always pushing the rules to the limit. But they seemed to get away with their raucous misdoings, the chef d'equipe and team trainer putting their antics down to 'boyish behaviour'. Georgie didn't dare step out of line, not for a second, for fear she would be sent home in disgrace. She was just so relieved to be on this team in the first place.

The third boy was the quietest, Simon. His parents were divorced, and it was usually his mother, Lynne, who was at shows with him, helping to tack up the ponies, putting up the practice fence, and cooking meals in the horsebox at the end of the day.

Whatever, he was a really quiet rider, whose ability Georgie really admired. He might not have the best pony, but he certainly got the best out of what he rode.

The fourth boy had a pony Georgie had always admired and would have liked to own. He came from a true working-class family and defied many of the odds to make it to this level.

Sean was difficult to know and, she suspected, a little simple, but he rode with nerves of steel, and his parents had fought long and hard to get him to where he was, giving up a lot to ensure they could pay the bills that allowed him to compete on the national circuit and 'get noticed'.

Robbie, Davey and Simon had all ridden-on teams before. Their family pony backgrounds had seen them ride on the Home Pony Internationals on many occasions – competitions where four riders from each of Scotland, Ireland, England and Wales would take on one another for the championship title.

They'd also ridden abroad. Their family pedigree ensured they received prized invitations from show owners across Europe to compete in sought-after events. To them this was 'just another show'. To Georgie it was her life. Her dream.

As they arrived at the port to join the queues of waiting traffic, Georgie could see the water outside the safety of the harbour was rough. A large yacht was pitching wildly as it hit the top of the waiting breakers. As soon as she heard the sound of the oak against her window that morning, she knew they were in for a storm.

The Chef d'Equipe, Lorraine, came up to the box. "Sorry Mark, you're going to have to go up to the stables and unload for a while. They aren't taking any livestock at the moment, it's too rough."

The two grooms travelling in the box, her own Lizzie and another girl Jenny, knew they were going to have work to do, to settle their charges into another strange yard while they waited for the winds to drop. The riders and parents were told they could wait, or cross, and continue to Hagen where hotel rooms were waiting.

A vote was taken and the riders decided to stay with their horses. It was a long wait, spent in the café and sea front amusement parks until night fell and the sea calmed. At 7pm they got the call, the ponies were loaded and returned to the port.

Following the box into the huge mouth of the P&O ferry, Georgie was fascinated to see how they attached chains to each wheel, securing the lorry to the deck. They left space behind, lowering the ramp for extra ventilation during the crossing, and Georgie could see Allie looking all round, completely nonplussed, just interested in all the goings on.

Jumping on the lorry and squeezing between the partitions, she snuggled up to Allie's warm flank, as much to give herself confidence, as to reassure her pony. "We're really on the way now girl," she said. "No turning back. Just chill, we've quite a journey ahead, then a rest day before the vetting and the real competition begins."

Allie leaned against her, as if sensing her young riders' uncertainty. She knew exactly what was going on. She had crossed rougher stretches of water in her life – especially the Irish Sea – and was already standing full square, leaning on the partitions to brace herself as the ship pitched.

After some 40 minutes the children could spot the lights of Calais twinkling through the darkness ahead.

Entering the harbour the engines slowed, the pitching stopped, and other travellers woke up from their gentle slumbers, most preparing for long night drives ahead.

After a customs check for horses and riders – each pony has to have its own international passport which carries a full description, supplied by a vet, and a record of all foreign shows attended – the convoy was on its way. Travelling in the night did have its advantages, as there was little traffic, and the group finally hit the town of Hagen close to 2am in the morning.

The riders were sent straight to their hotel, the grooms dispatched to unload and stable the ponies, under the watchful eyes of the team officials. Georgie had never been so pleased to see her bed, and quickly realized the advantage of being the only girl – she had a room with its own bathroom, all to herself. They boys were sharing two other rooms on the same corridor.

Hanging her riding clothes in the nearby wardrobe she decided the rest of her unpacking could wait until the morning. She had to meet the others for breakfast at 9am, and wanted to get some sleep so she was fresh. As soon as her head hit the pillow she was out like a light.

Woken by the telephone next to her bed ringing loudly in her left ear, she realized she had less than 20 minutes to shower and get dressed and make breakfast. Running down the stairs, exactly 18 minutes later, she saw the others already seated at a table looking out on to a cobbled courtyard.

Helping herself to some cereal and toast, she sat down next to Lorraine who was running through the itinerary for the day.

"We'll leave for the showground at 9.30, and I want you all to look smart. Not show breeches, yard breeches will do, not leggings or jeans. Ride for an hour in the sand school or on the grass, just to loosen the ponies up, they've had quite a long journey, and need to get moving.

"I'll watch each one carefully and make sure they're moving well. The vetting starts at 4pm, and we need to get the whole team through in one piece. So, don't work too hard, lots of walking and trotting on a long rein, just to get the muscles nice and relaxed. Tomorrow morning, before the first competition, we'll put in some proper warming up work."

Bounding back up the stairs Georgie slipped on her work breeches and half chaps, and was back in the lobby ready to board the minibus. She couldn't wait to see the showground, and the stables she'd heard so much about.

The facility at Hagen was owned by the Kassleman family, famous for their production of dressage horses around the world, and home of the annual PSI sales, that often produced record prices for performance horses across all disciplines. All the riders had been looking forward to this visit.

As the bus drove under the welcoming timber-framed archway, Georgie could see horses everywhere, all around her, hundreds of them. They were being ridden in the ménages that flanked either side of the drive, were turned out in small, railed paddocks full of dark green grass, being led along cobbled walkways that intersected the grounds, or being ridden along grass bridleways that led towards welcoming woodland she could see on the horizon.

The overall impression was one of organisation, neatness, style, quality and contentment. Everyone seemed to know exactly what they were doing, and why. The horses, and riders, seemed to have a happy purpose. She had never seen anywhere like it in her life.

Pulling up outside one of the long lines of indoor stables, Georgie noticed a British flag hanging proudly outside. Next to it were the French, Irish, Dutch, Italian, Swedish and Belgian flags. All were gently fluttering in the light breeze.

Walking into the block she was amazed by how large, airy and spacious each stable was.

Brick-built, they had solid wooden doors, each holding a bronze panel into which a name, country and riders' details had been placed. Soon she came across the five British ponies, all together, all five heads expectantly waiting their riders.

It was the first time she had seen it, proof she was

now part of the British squad:

No.42

April Days.

Great Britain.

Rider: Georgie Stones.

And there was Allie, looking every inch the star, all tacked up, ready to ride.

"Right, let's get sorted and out into the arena," barked Lorraine. "We have arena 3 to ourselves for an hour, so let's make the most of it, and make sure all these ponies have travelled well."

All riders were legged up and girths checked. Robbie's pony led the way out into the sunlit arena, and quickly started to prance around, eager to let off steam. Allie was, as always, the perfect lady, taking in her surroundings with casual interest, then settling down to listen to Georgie's instructions.

Lorraine and team trainer Gerald took in each pony's movement carefully. They couldn't afford to lose one of the team at the vetting later that afternoon, and two of the ponies picked were quite old now. Although sound, a long journey could stiffen them up, and it was important that work loosened the muscles before the all-important trot-up.

Allie felt good, and Georgie sighed in relief. She'd been worried she might feel different after nearly two days on the road, with the unexpected delay in Dover. As if to prove her right, the mare suddenly leapt to the side as a bird scuttled out of a tree and flew across the ménage, almost brushing her head. Throwing in a joyful buck and a squeal, Georgie felt herself lose a stirrup as she struggled to sit tight.

The work done, and all five ponies pronounced fit and sound, the two grooms set to work washing, grooming and plaiting the quintet for the vetting at 4pm. The riders were taken into the pretty flower-filled village for lunch, before returning to the hotel to change. They had to wear their show breeches, jackets, hats and boots for the occasion – this being the start of the weekend's activities. The show wasn't deemed to start until the vetting had been completed.

Just before 4pm the riders were assembled outside the stables. "You all know the form, we've practiced this before," said Lorraine. "Stand on the near side of your pony, the left, and hold the reins, over the pony's head, in your left hand, with your right hand a little higher.

"You'll be on a long flat surface and you will see the three vets with a table and someone taking notes at the end.

"When your number is called you must run, with your pony trotting, towards them in a straight line. When you reach the table you must halt, let them check the pony against the FEI passport they hold and, when they tell you to go, turn and run back. This way they see the pony's action from the front and the back on a hard surface. If they see any unsoundness, they will stop the pony from competing."

Georgie knew it was also possible that they would call a pony to one side for measuring. Ponies were only ponies if they were 148cms, or 14.2hh, or less. The FEI stuck to very rigid rules here, and often ponies were 'measured out'. Allie had a life height certificate, meaning she had been measured twice, in consecutive years, and each time been under the set limit – but it didn't stop her being measured again if someone thought she looked too big.

The five riders joined the long line of competitors waiting their turn. With 11 teams entered, there were 55 ponies to check, five from each nation. They watched anxiously and saw two ponies 'spun', one from the French team that had struck into itself badly travelling, and was clearly lame on its front nearside, the other, an older Spanish pony, that just looked stiff. The Spanish pony could be re-presented for a second chance the following day.

Allie started to jog on the spot, getting impatient. Robbie and his grey went first. 'Pass'. Next was Davey, with his bay. 'Pass'. Now it was Georgie's turn. She set off at a run, Allie obediently trotting by her side. Standing by the desk, while the vets checked her passport, she realised they were smiling at her, recognising the pony she held. 'OK, trot back' she was told. As she got back to the Chef d'Equipe she heard the magic word 'Pass'. Simon and Sean followed, and also heard the all-important word 'Pass'.

Leaving the grooms to untack, feed and settle the ponies, the five went back to the hotel again, this time to shower and get dressed in the team uniform, ready for the opening reception being held in a huge marquee back on the showground. For Georgie this meant a white shirt, dark blue blazer with shiny brass buttons, red scarf and blue skirt, with a narrow split up the side. The boys had similar shirts and blazers, with a red tie, and smart dark blue pants.

A long and low wolf whistle drew her attention as she came out of her bedroom. "Hey Georgie, that get up really suits you – shows off those legs," said Davey, trying to wind her up. "Just shut up and behave," she replied. "And remember we aren't allowed to drink. Just for once do things right. We've got a lot at stake in the next few days."

She heard him chuckle under his breath and knew both boys thought she was a stick-in-the mud, too prim and proper. She knew how to have fun, there was no doubt about that, but she wasn't one of the many teenagers on the circuit willing to sleep around, or tumble into a physical relationship for the sake of it. Her only really bad habit was smoking, and as she was careful not to let her parents find out, she would quietly puff away when no-one was about.

As the bus pulled back up at the showground, she could hear the latest music coming from the lit marquee. The path up to it was flanked by glowing torches and, as each team was asked to come forward to be presented, their National Anthem was played.

It seemed the whole of the nearby village had been invited, and that there were more than 300 people inside. Guest of honour was the local Mayor, a heavy gold chain around his neck ensuring he stood out from the crowd.

All along one side of the marquee were trestle tables full of food. Everything you could imagine as every taste had been catered for. Fussy though she was, Georgie found she soon had a plate of food in front of her. As the evening wore on, various dignitaries were brought around and introduced, and time and time again she found she was introduced as the rider of the infamous April Days. It did nothing for her nerves.

As the bus took them back to the hotel later than night, Georgie was horrified to find two of the boys had been drinking. How, she wasn't sure, as no-one under the age of 16 was supposed to have been given alcohol. They could hardly stand up, and it was all the others could do to get them up the steps and into a seat.

This was the definite negative side of being on a team of boys. In some ways she was pleased to be 'one of them' and not excluded from their boyish pranks, but on the other she was horrified by their behaviour when they were abroad, representing their country, on a team.

She went to sleep that night fitfully, worrying about the state of the boys in the morning, and hoping they weren't going to feel too ill to compete. She was ready, as ready as she would ever be, and was determined to make the most of this opportunity she'd been given.

Chapter
6

The Competition

The Friday morning dawned bright and still. As she pulled back the curtains, Georgie saw the sun was shining, and there wasn't a cloud in the sky. A good omen, she hoped.

Her nerves were getting to her, she didn't feel hungry at all, but she forced down a few spoonful's of cereal, knowing she shouldn't compete on an empty stomach. She was amazed to see the two boys tucking into a man-sized fried breakfast of bacon, egg and German sausage.

The bus took them to the showground at 9am, and Lorraine took them across to the ring for a team talk.

"Right, you know how this goes. Your class is at 11 o'clock. The draw is as follows:

Sean, you are 4th to go, Simon, 13th, Georgie 22nd, Robbie 34th and Davey 50th. It's a one round speed class. No heroics. You're not here to win this class, you're here to ride for your country. The objective is to jump a clear round inside the time. To get your ponies settled. Let them see some of the fences, some of which will be in the team competition, and let them get used to the arena. I just want you all home safe. We are here for the team event on Sunday, not individual glory. Remember that.

"The course will be open for walking at 10am. Sean, you must be warmed up before you walk the course, then you'll have a chance to watch one go before you go in. The rest of you know the score.

"Simon, watch Sean and Georgie, Robbie and Davey watch until there are about 10 to go before you, then go into the collecting ring. We'll be there to help you at the practice fences."

Georgie walked round to the stables to see how Allie was doing. She looked stunning, Lizzie had done a marvelous job. Her mane was neatly plaited, her tail too, and her coat shone. Her headcollar with her name etched on the side was on, it was too early for her to be tacked up. Easing open the door, she walked into the airy stall.

"Well girl, this is it, this is what we're here for," she said. "You're going to have to help me out a bit today, I know you've done it all before. This is a first for me. I'll try not to let you down, but you have to look after me. This time we can't win, we just have to jump round clear."

Georgie knew how important it was to jump clear. Although there were five ponies and riders, only four would be in the team on Sunday. That meant one of them wouldn't ride for their country. To be that 5th rider was one of the hardest things to learn to deal with. She was terrified this could be her, so was determined to follow 'team' orders to the letter.

The class today was a warm-up for the Grand Prix on Saturday. And, after the Grand Prix, the team would be chosen, based on the results from these two classes. Georgie knew how tough it would be to be the one left out, and she was determined that wasn't going to be her. She already had the Union Jack badge sewn onto her show jacket, and she was determined she'd wear it because she had ridden on the team, not because she had travelled to Hagen.

The five walked the course together, carefully measuring the distances between each fence, and relating that to each pony's stride. The first thing she noticed was how flat the cups holding the poles were, and the lightness of the poles themselves. A pony would only have to brush the top for it to fall to the ground.

Then the fences themselves were quite different. They were modern, bright and airy, with few of the traditional fillers seen in England. There was a fence made to look like a bicycle, and a curved grey and bright yellow wall, something she had never seen before.

There were quite a few opportunities to take short

cuts, to turn inside one fence to another to make up valuable time, but Georgie knew she couldn't take those lines. Her job was to get through the start and finish inside the time.

Allie was always described as forward-going. What the phrase meant was that she got on a forward stride, and rarely had to be checked.

So, if there was a distance of four and a half strides from one fence to another, Allie would usually cover the ground in four, not have to be held to fit in five. Show jumping was actually quite a science, although those watching probably never noticed.

Simon's pony was one of the smaller ones, so he was instructed to put in strides, but to keep moving all the way round. The time allowed to complete each course is much shorter in international competitions, and it can be easy to pick up costly time faults.

Georgie walked the course twice, and then went to sit with the others, waiting for the class to begin. She began to feel very nervous and, as the first rider came into the ring and waited for the bell to signify that he could start, she felt her stomach churning.

"To start us off in this first speed competition is number 22, Phillipe Janin riding Belle Air for France," said the announcer, in English. She watched as Phillipe let his horse canter around the ring, come to a stop in front of the judges box and salute, and then, as soon the bell sounded, start to head towards the first fence.

As he went through the timing, the clock started ticking. She could see the seconds pass by as he made his way around the course. The first awkward distance was between fence three and four, either a long three from an upright to a double of oxers, or a short four.

He opted for the long three, and his pony kicked out the front bar of the first part of the double, then struggled to make the distance, knocking both top poles of the second part to the ground.

He started to slow a little, and Georgie could see how tight the time was. Deciding to gallop to the last, he got through the timing with just 0.5 second to spare. She knew she was going to have to keep moving all around this twisty track if she was to take the longer lines and not run up time faults.

Soon it was time for Sean. As a rider from Spain came towards the last line, she saw his dark bay pony enter the ring, ears pricked, prancing, and pulling at the bit, keen to get going.

"Fourth to go in this class is no 43, Sean Phillips riding My Magic Day for Great Britain." The bell rang, and off he set. Following the team instructions perfectly, he jumped a lovely round, with only a slight hesitation as he approached the unusual, curved wall. But a good kick had sent the pony forward, and although the thin bricks on the top moved, they stayed put. He was inside the time and went into the lead.

Georgie ran to the collecting ring. "Well done, Sean,

well done. That looked great," she said. "What's it like out there?"

Sean immediately told the other four riders how the course had ridden. He had put in an extra stride between fences three and four, realising that as they were on a bit of an uphill gradient, it was going to be hard, even with a forward-going pony, to make it in three. As a result, he had posted the first clear round. That early distance had been posing quite a problem for the first team members.

She went back to her place in the stands. Lizzie had brought Allie up to the collecting ring and was walking her quietly around. She wouldn't get on until there were about 10 to go before her name was called and reckoned she would jump on as soon as she had seen Simon's round.

The course was beginning to take its toll. Although not difficult, some of the distances were catching the riders out and most teams seemed to be letting their riders 'go for it'. Many of the short cuts were being tried, some without success, with rider after rider having a fence down. When Simon entered the ring, Sean was still in second place, with his relatively slow clear round.

"Next to go is number 45, Simon Minster riding Danny's Delight for Great Britain." The bell sounded and he was off. Georgie soon saw he was not following the team instructions, and gasped as he turned up short to the second fence. Danny was trying his best, his age and experience helping to give every fence room, but as he approached the curved wall, she could see he was backing off.

"Kick, ride him forward," Georgie said to herself, "don't lose it now." But Danny was uncertain. He didn't like the look of this wall at all. Simon put his leg on as hard as he could, his strength aimed at getting the pony over the brightly coloured wall. To her surprise he jumped it, from almost a standstill, but paid the penalty by taking three of the top bricks with him as he scraped over the top.

She could sense the disappointment in the crowd. Up to that point it looked like a winning round. Running to the collecting ring she was in time to hear the mixed message from Lorraine. "Well ridden Simon, now we know you're going to have to ride strong at that wall tomorrow, but at least he has jumped it. But what were you doing? Your orders were to jump a solid safe clear."

Walking towards Allie, she didn't hear his reply, but knew he wouldn't be in serious trouble. He had come home safe and had wanted to win. What could be wrong with that?

Lizzie gave her a leg up, and she could feel the pent-up tension in the mare beneath her. She wanted to get on with her job. Warming up slowly, she was surprised to see Lorraine come into the middle of the arena to help with the jumps. They followed the usual set pattern – an upright on one side of the collecting ring, an oxer on the other.

Waiting for the upright to start as a cross pole, Georgie came into the fence, full of confidence. Allie hopped over it, with disdain, giving the familiar buck the other side.

Digging her heels into her side Georgie said: "We'll have none of that young lady. We're here to do a job today, not mess about. Concentrate."

As the vertical got higher, Georgie sensed the concentration coming, and switched to the oxer which alternated from being an ascending fence – one where the front pole would be lower than the back – to a square one, where both front and back poles would be level, making it harder to judge the distance of the back one.

The fence was wider and higher than anything inside the class and, just before the collecting ring steward called her number, she popped a last vertical, this time a single pole designed to make the mare think.

As the rope was moved away, Georgie trotted into the ring, keeping to the right to stay out of the line of the pony just finishing the course. Suddenly she was on auto pilot, not even hearing her name called out over the loudspeaker, but realizing the crowd had gone silent. You could hear a pin drop. People had stopped talking and were making their way to the arena to see this pair compete.

She heard the bell ring, put her hand up to her hat to push it down tight, gathered her reins and set off. Riding forward from the start, she came to the first vertical on a perfect stride. Feeling the mare's confidence beneath her, Georgie decided to turn short to the second. Allie rose to the challenge and cleared the fence easily, eating up the ground up the hill to the third. Safely over that she landed half a stride out, so pushed for the three up the hill to the oxer. Clear.

Turning the corner she rode fast at the triple bar, a fence that looked imposing, but one Allie always loved. Still clear they steadied for the bicycle fence, clearing it by a long way. Coming to the combination, Georgie started to relax, and felt the mare look at the line ahead, judging the distance between the three fences. She cleared them easily and turned towards the curved grey and yellow wall that had so unsettled Simon earlier.

Giving her an unnecessary kick, Allie jumped forward, and suddenly Georgie realised she was going to have to take a pull to get in the four strides. Her pony responded immediately, the takeoff spot was perfect, the wall cleared. With just three fences to go, she turned inside to the final line, saving valuable seconds.

The two oxers and final vertical were cleared with ease, and she leant forward, galloping through the timing. As she sat up to pull the mare up, she heard the announcer say: "and we have a new leader, Georgie Stones for Great Britain riding April Days."

Her time was two seconds faster than her nearest rival, but her happiness short-lived.

"What did you think you were doing," shouted Lorraine. "None of you seem to be listening today. You were supposed to ride for a steady clear."

Simon and Sean came up to her and congratulated her, telling her to ignore Lorraine's anger. "She was smiling a few minutes ago, she just has to be seen to say the right thing," they reassured her.

Walking the pony off, she acknowledged the congratulations from some of the foreign riders she hadn't yet got to know. She was busy patting Allie when a large German man came up to her and introduced himself.

Puffing on a large cigar he said: "I'm Henrich Hasselhoff, my son is one of the German team riders, and I want to buy your pony," he said. "Well, she is not for sale," responded Georgie, smiling with confidence. "You will not decide this, you do not own her," was his quick reply. "I own the country's largest chain of supermarkets, and I'm going to buy her for my son to take him to the Europeans. I will go and find the owner, your mother no?"

Still smiling at his arrogance, Georgie turned away. Jumping down from Allie, she ran up the stirrups, loosened the girth and put on her sweat rug. Now she had to watch the rest of the class and wait. Lizzie started to walk her off, while Georgie sat nervously in the stands. She really wanted a place in her first international class, even if it was a lower one.

Robbie was next to go, on the grey mare his parents had bought in Norway. She could have flashes of sheer brilliance, but could also be very spooky, and Georgie knew both the wall and the bicycle fence could pose a threat. But, thankfully, the mare was fully on-song and cleared the course with ease. Robbie too, as usual, ignored team instructions and galloped round the speed class, easily taking over the lead.

To her frustration Georgie saw there was nothing but smiles and congratulations for him as he entered the collecting ring. Why was it he was never told off for breaking the rules? Was it because of his parents, or because he was a boy, or because he'd been in the game for such a long time? She didn't know, but knew whatever the reason, it was totally unfair.

Keeping her place in the stands she saw several other riders move in front of her, but none went as fast, and clear, as Robbie. Then it was Davey's turn. What would he do?

Coming into the ring on a long rein, Davey seemed completely confident and at ease, taking everything in his stride... if he was nervous, it certainly didn't show. Hearing the crowd clap as his name was called, he cantered towards the first fence.

His bay gelding had seen it all before and tackled the course with ease. Not looking like touching a pole, they came home a second slower than Georgie, and three seconds slower than Robbie, but in a good enough time to finish 10th.

When the final results were read, it was a win for Robbie, fourth for Georgie, 10th for Davey, 16th for Sean and 28th for Simon with his four faults. Together they had put in a good show. Just the top eight were called into the ring for the presentations, and to her surprise there were no rosettes, but medals instead, and rugs for the first three ponies.

"Never mind girl, we'll get a rug in the Grand Prix tomorrow," she said to the mare. "We'll show them what we can really do when the fences go up. You'll come into your own then, I know."

Chapter
7

Disaster Strikes

Saturday morning dawned bright and warm, and Georgie started to realise how nervous she was when she couldn't face any breakfast at all. Her stomach was churning and she noticed as she went to take a mouthful of tea that her hands were shaking.

"Pull yourself together," she whispered to herself. "Now's not the time to get nervous."

Under the watchful eye of Lorraine she somehow managed to force down a slice of toast, wondering how the boys were managing to clean their plates of a greasy fried egg and bacon breakfast, especially as she knew they had sneaked out into the town the previous night and met up with some of the Swedish girls.

They were leaving for the showground early as Lorraine wanted all the ponies to have a 20 minute schooling session before the Grand Prix, and she wanted plenty of time for her young team to see the course built and to walk it at least twice.

As the minibus pulled into the yard she could see

Lizzie waiting with a very anxious look on her face. "Oh God, please don't let anything have happened to Allie," she prayed.

She was last to clamber off the bus and saw Lorraine walk quickly to Lizzie. After a few minutes of hushed conversation, she called Sean over. Georgie pushed through the other riders to hear what was wrong.

"Sean, there's been a bit of an accident." Immediately seeing the young boys' concern, she said "it's alright, nothing to panic about, but Magic struck into himself during the night, must have got caste, and he has a bit of a cut on his near front heel. Lizzie has done her best, and has been hosing it most of the morning so, before you jump on, let's trot him up on a hard surface and see how he goes."

Georgie was immediately aware of mixed feelings. While she felt terribly sorry for Sean, she was also aware that, if his pony were unsound, she would definitely be on the team, however she did today. Then she felt really bad for thinking of benefiting, even for a second, from someone else's bad luck.

She walked over the Sean and put her arm on his shoulder. "Would you like me to come with you," she asked. "I'm sure he will be OK; Lizzie is really good at this sort of thing."

Sean looked at her and smiled. "Yes, thanks, I've waited so long to get this far, I just want a chance to show the selectors what I can do," he said.

Together they walked across the flower filled yard and into the British team's block of indoor stables. They saw Magic led out of his stall and heaved a huge sigh of relief... he looked sound.

Following Lizzie and Lorraine outside, the concern was palpable. No-one was talking. No team, favourites or not, wanted to lose one of their team members before the start of the Nations Cup.

Georgie stood with Sean as Magic was trotted up and down, twice. He did seem a little tender on his near fore but, as another pony went to walk by him he stopped, threw up his head and started prancing on the spot, showing off in a way only he could.

Lizzie struggled to keep hold of him and wished she had him in a bridle, not the headcollar she had hastily used. "Nothing much wrong with how he is feeling," she said to Lorraine.

Both groom and trainer ran their hands over the cut. There was no heat, and he didn't flinch when pressure was applied. "Sean," called Lorraine. "I think he'll be fine. Let's put him back in the box and not work him this morning. You're late to go in the class so he's got at least another four or five hours to rest before he has to work. Lizzie, take him out and hose him again in another two hours' time."

Georgie was so relieved for Sean and saw the colour slowly coming back into his face.

"Right, everyone else, get tacked up and let's go out

onto the grass next to the main arena," said Lorraine. "I want to see these ponies do some proper work so they're not too fresh this afternoon."

Once again Georgie was amazed by the beauty of her surroundings as she popped up on the mare and walked quietly along the cobbled roads that took her to the practice arena. There were hanging baskets full of colourful blooms everywhere she looked, window boxes on the back of all the stall windows, immaculately cut grass with neat border edges, and some of the most beautiful equine sculptures she had ever seen.

Getting into her usual warm-up routine she could feel how well Allie felt beneath her. She cast her mind back to how much she had hated the mare when she arrived and realised, again, how long it took to build the special relationships that took you to the top. There were always huge discussions about how much of a successful partnership was the rider and how much the horse or pony.

Many times she'd felt she was merely a passenger, Allie was so exceptional. But, in her heart, she knew that wasn't true. People might think the pony was a push button ride, but she was far from it. Georgie had to ride the mare to the best of her ability, ensuring she hit the right spot every time, giving Allie the maximum opportunity to clear the huge fences she was going to face. It took dedication, commitment and skill.

After 30 minutes of walk, trot and canter, with some tight circles and shortening and lengthening of stride, it was time to put her back into the stable, give her a small feed, and go for lunch. While she was riding, she'd been only too aware of the imposing figure of Henrich Hasselhoff leaning on the white post and rail fence. She saw him turn away as she made her way back to the stables and try to catch up with her mother who was already making her way to the picnic area.

She was as confident as she could be that her mother would turn down any offer, however large. She was in it for the long haul, just like her grandfather and father.

Lizzie took Allie from her as they reached the yard and told her she was going to give her a bath to make sure her coat gleamed in the afternoon sun. A groom's work was never done and now there was a bath to organise before the mare was walked dry with a sweat rug to stop her from catching a chill, then last minute trimming, plaiting her mane and tail, and some quiet relaxing for a couple of hours before tacking her up for the Grand Prix. Then, while Allie was chilling, Lizzie would be cleaning and checking all the tack, making sure it was in top condition.

Her mother was sitting at one of the picnic tables by the time Georgie had crossed to the other side of the facility – the tables spread out on a slight hill overlooking the large ring where already the course was being built.

"That man is so arrogant," she said to Georgie. "Thinks he can wave his big cheque book around and we'll fall over to sell the mare. He's offered a huge amount of money, as long as she passes a full vetting with scans and x rays from his choice of vet, nearly double what we paid for her, but I've told him she's not for sale. I don't think he believes me... just thinks I'm trying to increase the price!"

Inwardly Georgie heaved a huge sigh of relief. She'd been fairly confident her mother would refuse any offer, but to hear the words spoken so confidently, made her leap up and give her mother a spontaneous hug. Top ponies were often on the market for the right price – mainly for fear of an injury ending their competition life – but there was no way Georgie wanted to see her European Championship dreams collapse for the sake of a large wad of money. There would be no way Allie could be replaced, however substantial the offer. There just wasn't another pony like her.

Gradually the other team members and families came over to join them and they all enjoyed a picnic hamper put together by the show organisers. There were warm rolls, cheese, a selection of German meats, fruit, cool drinks and, for those with the appetite, a pot of chocolate mousse.

The conversation centred around everyone's hopes

for the afternoon, the desire to make 'the team' and a look at the competition, with Germany, the home nation, strong favurites to win the following day's Nations Cup.

Gradually the riders made their way back to the stables to get changed into their show gear and got ready to walk the course. Keeping quietly to herself, Georgie started to focus on the afternoon ahead. She knew the course would be demanding, and much bigger than the previous days' speed class, but also had total confidence in her mare.

It was so difficult for Georgie to explain how intelligent her mount was. She remembered the time a couple of weeks earlier when she had woken up to the sound of hoofbeats passing her bedroom window. Shocked to hear a loose horse on the road outside, she had run to her bedroom window just in time to see Allie clear a 3ft garden gate, right next to the greenhouse, canter across the concrete yard, and jump a steel 5-bar gate into her usual field.

She'd been horrified but, at the same time, full of admiration for the ability of her pony. Earlier that morning Lizzie had taken Allie up the road to a field they were renting from some neighours. Clearly Allie had decided she wasn't staying up the road in an unfamiliar field on her own and had made her own way back to the house. Before she even got to the main road she'd jumped two post and rail fences then, by all accounts, carefully cantered along the edge of the narrow lane, avoiding the morning rush hour traffic, before turning into her home drive.

To top it all, she was wearing her sponsor, Horseware's, heavy Rambo rug, and when she was safely back in her usual paddock, turned round to look at Georgie leaning out of her bedroom window as if to say "huh, that'll teach you, I'm not staying up the road on my own."

Georgie smiled at the memory and knew few people would ever understand just how special this mare was. It wasn't just her desire to win, or her naked ability – it was her intelligence and understanding that made her so different.

As the months had passed, the whole family had fallen in love with this mare and had never seen a need to heighten the fencing in the home paddocks. Allie had settled into her new surroundings as if she'd been there every day of her life and had never attempted to jump out.

She was woken from her reverie by the sound of a bell, signifying the start of walking the course. In a group with her other compatriots, led by Lorraine, they set off towards the first fence, an upright on an angle, facing straight into the grandstand which would be packed with supporters moving around.

Six forward strides took the group to another upright, followed on a dog leg to an ascending oxer.

Fence four was at the top of the ring, a parallel with a wide water tray underneath. The bicycle fence was back again as fence five, followed by the curved wall which now looked even more spooky as some of the bricks had been removed from the bottom, leaving it gappy and open.

Next up was the double, a vertical followed on two long strides by a wide oxer at maximum height and then a run down the hill towards the open water.

Five more strides led to a vertical, again at maximum height, and then the triple bar. Turning for home, it was uphill to the planks and five strides to a final double, this time an ascending one as the first part, followed by a true oxer.

It was a long and twisting course and was unusual not to have a treble, but the two doubles instead. Georgie knew there were some tricky strides, but there was nothing that particularly worried her. Although big, the course was smaller than some she had ridden in England, so she felt confident as she went to watch the first few go. She hadn't been so lucky with the draw this time and would be the first of her team to go – 10th into the ring – so she had time to watch two before she had to jump on.

To her surprise both of the first riders had the first fence down. Perhaps they were distracted with movement in the crowds or perhaps it was the handicap of having an up-to-height vertical as the first fence which was catching a few of the less experienced riders out.

Warming up in the sand arena, she made sure to jump a large vertical as the last fence before she entered the ring. Then it was her turn... this time she was the pathfinder and, as she heard the ring steward call her forward, she moved up to the rope separating the collecting ring from the jumping arena.

Again she heard the hush as her name boomed out over the loudspeaker. Saluting to the judge's box, she got Allie into a collected canter and she looked for her line to the first fence and felt the joy as she soared over the top, not even rubbing the highest pole.

Time seemed to stand still as she made her way around the course. There had been only one clear round from the first nine riders, and Georgie could feel she was going to be the second. Galloping over the water she felt safe and calm inside, knowing some of the harder parts of the course were behind her.

The planks were three from home, this time light and airy, and painted blue with wavy lines, looking like the sea. As her mare easily cleared the fence she felt her left leg fly loose, away from her flank, and realised to her horror that her stirrup leather had broken.

She had no time to think. They were four strides from the final fence, the double. Coming to it up the hill, Georgie realised they were short and kicked the mare forward, urging her closer to the fence. Unsettled by this sudden instruction, Allie twisted in the air, completely unbalancing Georgie who ended up on her neck.

Hearing the bar hitting the ground behind her, it took all her balance and experience to stay aboard as the mare picked up for the second fence. Unbalanced she knew the mare had no chance, and indeed heard the second pole fall too. Eight faults.

She managed to stay on through the finish and made it to the collecting ring. The stirrup was brought to her by one of the fence judges – it had hit the ground between the two elements of the double.

Lorraine made her way across the collecting ring and took Georgie to one side. She didn't spare her words. "Broken tack is a beginners mistake. Did you check the leathers this morning?" Not waiting for a reply, she carried on: "You'll go home from the show and practice riding and jumping without stirrups for as long as it takes you to be able to jump this mare without unbalancing her or falling off. You were lucky to stay on and made a real mess of today. It simply isn't good enough. You let your pony down by making a simple mistake. There's no room for mistakes on my team."

As soon as she could Georgie ran away. Away from her team members, away from her mother, away from her groom, away from everyone. Finding a quiet spot on the other side of the showground she burst into an uncontrollable flood of tears. Her team chances were gone. She might have the British flag on the front of her jacket, but what right did she really have to wear it? She wasn't going to represent her country.

Her mother found her lying on the grass, tears streaming down her face. It was one of those moments when she really couldn't find the right words to console her. She knew how much this Grand Prix had meant to her and knew the pony had been jumping out of her skin. And deep down she knew the fault was Lizzie's, as much as it was Georgie's, it was their job to check the tack and surely both of them would have noticed a cracking leather when they cleaned the tack and checked it over?

Nothing she said seemed to be able to stem the river of tears. The worst of it was, she knew that somehow, she had to get Georgie back to the ringside as quickly as possible, it was considered very bad form not to watch your fellow competitors jump. And of course, going back to applaud the clear rounds, was the last thing in the world her daughter wanted to do.

"Come on Georgie, you have to pull yourself together. This is just one step backwards, and a small one at that, in a career that is just beginning. You have so many good times ahead and so many classes and medals to win. Right now, you have to prove to Lorraine that you are built of the right stuff, that you have the right character to take the knocks.

"This is why women get the short straw in this sport. Boys don't cry when this happens, they take it in their stride and move on. You have to show everyone you can do the same."

She watched her words sink in and allowed herself a small smile as Georgie sat up and asked for a handkerchief to dry her eyes. Together they walked back across the grass and got back to the ringside as the second British rider, Davey, was about to enter the ring.

He looked across at her and gave her a thumbs up and wink before he cantered into the ring, making his way to the judge's box. As she sat down with the other team members, she found that Sean had had an unlucky 4 faults at the water, and picked up two time faults, finishing on a score of six.

Georgie crossed her fingers as Davey approached the first fence. She realised she wanted him to do well... after all, he was riding for her country. After a nerve-jangling rattle at the triple bar, she watched him gallop through the finish just two seconds inside the time, posting only the fourth clear of the competition.

Three riders later and it was the turn of Simon. He also cantered into the ring, looking totally confident, but Georgie could see him tense as he started toward the first vertical. Halfway round the course disaster struck. Coming towards the curved wall, one of the course officials walked towards its sides, seeing the movement, Danny spooked, ran to the left, and despite a valiant effort, Simon couldn't get him straight enough to attempt the wall.

He did a circle, giving himself plenty of space and then really dug his heels in, giving the sandy coloured pony a smack down the neck to remind him who was boss. This time he jumped clear, but four faults and time faults, had put him out of the running.

So far, three British riders gone, and just the one clear round. The Germans had notched up three, the French and Dutch two apiece. The course was certainly taking its toll.

Next to go was Robbie, as usual the cockiest of the group, cantering into the ring and lifting his arm to salute the judges as if he had been under this pressure all his life.

Watching him go Georgie felt herself almost willing him to make mistakes. She knew at the moment she had the highest score and, unless Robbie had three fences down, she was certain she'd be dropped from the team. She couldn't bear to watch as he cleared fence after fence and realising he was just two from home, shut her eyes as he headed uphill.

The applause made her snap them open seconds later, just in time to see him punch the air in triumph – Britain's second clear round. She felt the tears begin to form in the corners of her eyes and made a dash to the toilets before anyone could spot her distress.

Last of the British quintet was Sean. She knew he was nervous and had tried to give him some support in the collecting ring. It would be the biggest track he and his pony had jumped and he really wanted to go well.

All was well until they got to the open water. Half a stride out to hit the wide jump accurately, Georgie saw the pony had put his foot on the tape. Both water judges stood up and signaled with a small flag... four faults. A good round for a first attempt under this pressure.

After the course had been shortened and heightened she found she had to sit and watch the boys fight it out. The course had certainly taken its toll – only seven clears from the 54 starters. She didn't care who won, all she wanted to do was run to her room and hide, knowing that once the class was over the team would be announced and she'd be the one left off. The one girl who travelled and, obviously, the weakest link...

Lizzie came and sat next to her in the grandstand, feeling the same anxiety as the jump off started. Neither of them could feel any real joy as Robbie jumped double clear and ended third and Davey had just the last fence down and came fifth. It seemed to them both that their long trip had ended in disappointment and sadness.

After the main ring presentations, and the three national anthems, Lorraine called her five riders together.

"This is always one of the hardest parts of my job," she said, "and you all know that one of you has to be dropped from the team competition tomorrow. I must admit the decision has been harder than usual as we didn't get the results we quite expected over the past two days, but I expect you all to accept my decision with grace and support each other tomorrow.

"Remember, we came here to win the Nations Cup and, although the Germans are firm favourites after their first and second places in the Grand Prix, I believe we have the pony power to take the trophy home."

Looking down at her handwritten notes she continued: "First to go will be Robbie, then Davey, Georgie you will be third – the most important place in the team – and Sean you will be fourth. I'm sorry Simon, but this time you will have to sit it out. You've already ridden on a British team, we know you can take the pressure, it's time for some others to have a chance. It's also been a long and tiring journey for Danny – at 19 he's the oldest pony on the team."

Georgie couldn't believe her ears. She looked at Lorraine and said: "Did you just say I was on the team? Am I really riding tomorrow?"

Smiling Lorraine replied: "Yes, Georgie, I did. Your track record with Allie this year is incredible. You have been almost unbeatable indoors and out. There's no way we would drop you from the team because of one bad round – anyway, eight faults in a Grand Prix is hardly a bad round. You also lack experience at this level, we need to get you in the ring, in a key position, to see how you deal with the pressure."

Georgie glanced across at Simon and could see he didn't look too upset. In her view he was already a dead cert for the Europeans, so she could see it made sense to try out some other potential partnerships. She also knew his pony would be tired after the travelling and, if he was to be kept on top form for the next three months, he needed to be well looked after.

Walking back to the stables to share the news with Allie, Georgie put her arm through her mother's. "What a long way we've come, Georgie. Your grandfather will be so proud when we ring him and give him the news. He told me the other day he was applying for a passport so he was ready to travel to the Europeans... I didn't have the heart to tell him that this year they were at Hartpury in Gloucestershire! Have you rung your dad yet?"

"Gosh, no, in all the excitement I quite forgot. I'll run and get my phone now. Dad will be so happy. I just wish he could have been here to watch tomorrow. Still, we'll have the video camera so we can watch it on TV when we get home next week."

Watching her daughter as she went skipping off to the lorry, barely able to contain her happiness, Jane mulled over how much can change in a couple of hours

– remembering the unnecessary streams of tears earlier that afternoon.

Not for the first time she recognized that sport at this level had the sorts of highs and lows it would be very difficult to anyone outside it to understand. And she recognised the pressure these young children faced when their only passion was to represent their country and win.

Chapter
8

The Nations Cup

Sunday morning dawned bright and clear, with just a light wind rustling the branches. Georgie had slept like the proverbial log, despite falling asleep imagining all sorts of misfortunes besetting her team. She saw it like that now... her team.

She went to her wardrobe and pulled out her best (and lucky) pair of breeches. She had been wearing this same pair when she won the last indoor Paul Fabrications qualifier of the season – the win that had put her up at the top of the table and ensured she was the British indoor champion. While not overly superstitious, she wasn't taking any chances today!

Pulling black leggings on over the breeches, she went down to breakfast, pleased to see she was the first to arrive. Helping herself to fruit and cereal from the buffet, she sat by a window, watching the sparrows flying in and out of the bird bath just outside the window.

"Feeling nervous yet sexy?" questioned Davey as he

pulled a chair from the adjacent table and set it next to her. "Allie has done this so many times you don't have to worry about a thing. Carlos isn't too happy with that wall, and spooks at anything, so I've really got to be on top of my game today."

Not for the first time Georgie felt the anger welling – why did everyone assume Allie was a push-button ride? Yes, she had ability to spare, but staying on her over the massive fences was a huge challenge in itself.

She wished they had a pony world championship, like the senior one, where the top four riders after two days of fierce competition have to ride each other's horses over the same track. The overall winner, and world champion, is definitely the best rider on that day, having conjured up clear rounds from horses he or she has never sat on before.

"That would sort this out once and for all," she said to herself. "Allie would start her bucking between the fences and these boys would soon find themselves on the ground."

As the others came up and joined them, she realised Simon was the only one not wearing his riding gear, instead dressed in the 'uniform' the team had donned for the welcome function. "Are you OK?" she whispered. "Fine," he said. "This has probably turned out for the best, Jenny has just called to say Danny had a bit of colic in the night and she had to walk him about in the dark for a couple of hours. It would have been too risky to jump him today."

In no time at all Lorraine was calling her charges together and marshalling them on to the minibus. Checking they had everything they needed for the busy day ahead, she settled into the task of keeping them motivated, focused and confident about the task ahead.

The journey seemed to take no time at all. Suddenly they were driving into the show centre and pulling up outside the stables. Georgie ran straight to Allie's box and pulled out a packet of polos as she approached the mare. "We're going to win the Nations Cup today, Allie, you need to be on top form. I'm certainly not going to have a problem with my stirrup leathers and we're going to show them how it's done. The Germans may be favourites, but we'll show them who's best..."

Allie nuzzled the palm of her hand, gratefully licking and then crunching the peppermint treat. She always looked forward to getting spoilt with a handful both before and after she'd jumped.

Lorraine was walking around each box in turn, gently running her hands down each pony's legs, making sure there was no heat or swelling. Calling her riders together she gave them a team talk, aimed at ensuring they remained focused on the task at hand.

"This is what you have come to Hagen for," she began. "The honour of riding for, and representing, your country. It's something that few achieve, but something that everyone who's serious about competing in this sport wants. It's the pinnacle of your pony career, and while this might be a Nations Cup today, it could be a European Championships in a few months' time, and even an Olympics or World Championships in the future.

"Today you ride as a team. Put any other thoughts out of your mind. You're here to help and support one another. The first rider to go, our pathfinder, will come back and share his experience with the rest of you. Any issues you have with one another must be left behind in the hotel - you're here because you're the best, the best riders with the best ponies - and now you have a chance to show the rest of Europe just how good you are.

"Some of you have more experience than others. Don't worry if you feel nervous. That's a normal feeling to have. But when you ride into the ring, and go to the judge's box to salute, focus on the job ahead. You must concentrate on getting through the start and the finish. We can win today. We have the best team, and I have total confidence in each and every one of you. Let's take home the cup for Britain."

Georgie felt Robbie reach out for her hands as the four of them stood in a small circle, holding hands and wishing each other luck, ending with 'high fives' all round. The start of the class might be two hours away, but the team spirit these youngsters shared was great to see. Lorraine smiled quietly to herself, confident she'd made the right choice.

Lorraine led the small group down to the grass bank overlooking the main arena where the final touches were being made to the course. As Georgie sat watching the flowers being put in place, she marvelled at how lovely the arena looked, closing her eyes and wanting to remember this moment forever.

The team were quick to spot some new and spooky fences. Everything had been built up to height, with the fences all very gappy and light, not like the more traditional fences at home. The bicycle fence had been replaced with two wagon wheels set side by side and the curved yellow wall now had multi-coloured bricks with lots of gaps in-between, meaning a pony approaching could see through the wall to the grass the other side.

The open water looked huge and there was only a small white picket fence in front of it. Already Georgie could spot one of the bogey fences as, a few strides later, stood a huge set of planks, the wavy blue ones that had caused some problems in an earlier class. Letting your pony gallop to stretch out over the water, then getting it back quickly to be back on its hocks for the planks, was going to be a challenge, especially as she could see the ground running downhill slightly between the two fences.

The group sat quietly, alone with their thoughts. Their parents were already sitting in the grandstand, having taken the opportunity to get in position early. They had the team sheets in front of them, seeing that Great Britain was fourth to go.

The rules for a Nations Cup are unique to this competition. Each country team has four riders and each rider must jump twice over exactly the same course. The best three scores in each round count.

So, in each round, one would be the discard score. Georgie was already determined this was not going to be her. Sometimes countries - such as Norway today - could only field three riders, perhaps a pony had been spun in the vet check or gone lame during one of the earlier competitions. These teams always started at a disadvantage, as every round counted, so a team with just three riders had no chance of removing a high-scoring round.

The start list showed that each 'first' rider for each country would jump, then the second rider, the third and the fourth. At the end of the first round all the scores would be totalled, with the discard score removed, and there would be an automatic team order for the second round. The team with the lowest number of faults would be jumping last, heightening the pressure.

At the end, should two teams end on the same number of penalty points, there would be a jump-off against the clock. But that rarely happened as, with eight rounds per team, there were plenty of opportunities for the light poles to fall. Nerves definitely played an important role, especially on a day like today, with lots of riders representing their country for the first time.

With half an hour before the course walk, Lorraine told her riders to go back to the stables, check all their gear carefully, put on their show breeches and jackets, and come back to the entrance into the arena from the collecting ring. It was a rule that the course was walked in full show gear and she was determined her team would shine from the start.

Georgie used the time to brush her hair through carefully, tying it into a neat ponytail and fastening the hairnet that would ensure it stayed inside her riding hat and couldn't fall into her eyes, taking off her leggings, zipping up her soft Sarm-Hippique boots, making sure her gloves were in her jacket pocket, also ensuring there was no dirt or dust on her navy show jacket.

She couldn't resist a last visit to Allie's stable. "I know you've done this before, but I haven't," she whispered. "Today you have to help me out. This is the first time you've represented Great Britain, and we have to make it count. I'll try my best not to let you down, we have to be a team today." Allie stretched her head towards Georgie and gently nickered, as if she understood her responsibility. Giving her a final pat, and a polo, Georgie left the stable, turning to see a knowing look in the mare's eye as she watched her young jockey walk away.

Not for the first time Georgie was left with the feeling that Allie understood everything and felt she was totally in charge.

Down by the ring she joined the boys who were already listening to Lorraine's sage advice. She realised all three of them were now taking this very seriously, all the usual banter and jocular teasing was gone. In its place, there was a desire to be part of a winning team.

The bell ringing to signify the start of the course walk shook her out of her reverie and she meekly followed the others into the ring. Listening carefully to Lorraine, and team trainer Gerald, she dutifully paced out the distances between fences and made a mental note of the lines she would take. As she approached the water at fence six, she was surprised to hear Robbie voice a concern. I'm not sure how Kiki will like this. The last time we had an open water like this was at Hickstead, and she ran out," he said.

Georgie had never heard Robbie express a concern for a particular jump before and wondered whether this was nerves or fact. "Yes, but you gave her a smack down the neck and she came to it willingly the second time," said Lorraine. "You have to expect open water like this at Nations Cup level. I'm sure you've practiced over it at home, and everything will be fine. Just come round the corner, don't give her too long to look at it, and ride at it as if you mean it."

Georgie could see Robbie was unsettled and went over to him to try and bolster his confidence. "Kiki will be fine, you ride her so well, and she's such a careful pony," she said, putting her hand on his shoulder. "Don't let what happened at Hickstead a couple of weeks ago stay inside your head. Be confident."

Robbie looked at her, the surprise showing in his face. "People think I don't get nervous because I come from a show jumping background. But sometimes that puts even more pressure on me," he confided. "If I ride it strong, she should be OK."

As they walked towards the planks, Georgie realised that her first observation about the distance from the open water to the plank vertical was right. It was downhill, meaning the ponies would still be very forward after being opened up for the water and the distance was a short five strides.

"This is going to be the testing part of the course," said Gerald. "Robbie you'll have to be careful here as you'll need to ride at the water, and Kiki isn't always the quickest to come back on the bridle. Make sure you don't make up too much ground, if anything, stand off the planks a little."

As they carried on around the long track it became clear that the treble combination, going uphill and away from the collecting ring, was also going to cause some problems.

It was a vertical in, one long stride to a big square oxer in the middle, and two short strides to a vertical out. "You can't come in too fast as you have a vertical in, but you need the momentum to jump the big oxer in the middle," said Gerald. "Luckily all of these ponies have scope to burn, so just stay on the same rhythm through and you'll be fine. Don't be tempted to push for the two strides, you'll land well out over the oxer, so sit up straight quick and let the fence come to you."

Out of the corner of her eye Georgie saw Sean walking the distance several times and thought he was concerned about Magic making up the distance to the final vertical. Magic was still relatively inexperienced at this level, so Sean was making certain he knew exactly how he was going to ride this tricky combination.

Having walked once with the chef d'équipe and team trainer, each of the riders walked the course again, lost in their own thought. Watching from the stands Jane felt for her young daughter and could only imagine the feelings washing over her as she walked from fence to fence.

She felt so powerless, yet knew she was best to leave Georgie in the hands of the professionals. Georgie had waited so long for this moment and Jane was so proud of what she'd achieved. Her partnership with Allie was cemented and she felt certain they would jump a double clear.

A few minutes later the bell rang again, the signal for the ring to be cleared, and for the first rider to be warming up in the collecting ring.

Robbie was the pathfinder, and fourth to go. He'd been warming Kiki up early so he could jump off and watch the first rider, a German. As the young Jan Hasselhoff, son of the arrogant supermarket owner entered the ring, there was a hushed silence, followed by raucous cheering and clapping when his name was announced. German flags were enthusiastically waved in the stands as Jan quietly patted his pony on the neck before cantering through the start.

In what seemed like hours, but was less than two minutes, Jan jumped around flawlessly, his pony looking to have wings as he made the course look so easy. What a start for the home nation. Georgie was sitting quietly in the rider section of the stand and thought what a good team the German's had. They badly wanted to win on home soil, but she was certain the Brits wanted to win more!

In no time at all she saw Robbie enter the ring on his prancing grey. He didn't look to have a care in the world as he saluted to the judges, but now she knew different. She crossed her fingers as he got into the canter rhythm that would take him round the course. Mentally she jumped every fence with him and saw him gather the reins and dig in his heels as he approached the water.

Just for a second it looked as though Kiki was going to sail across the open blue expanse. But suddenly time stood still as she stopped dead, right in front of the white picket fence, sending Robbie sailing through the air and depositing him unceremoniously into the dyed blue water.

As he got up, seemingly unscathed, she could see his breeches were blue from the dyed water, and worried as he approached Kiki, whip in hand. She knew about his sharp temper and prayed he would see common sense before he got back to his pony. The arena team were quick to catch Kiki and leg him back on board. The crowd clapped and he jumped a single fence before leaving the arena.

One fall and you are disqualified - the worst possible first round for Britain. It now meant, that whatever was yet to happen, Robbie's was the discount score. The pressure was now really on Davey, Georgie and Sean.

Georgie knew better than try and talk to Robbie. She knew what he must be feeling and knew she had to put that round behind her and concentrate instead on how she and Allie were going to make up for this unforeseen start.

Fences were falling all around the course, the planks after the water and combination taking their toll and, when the final rider from the first round had finished, there was just the one German clear. Sophie Hammeau for France on a lovely stallion called Le Vert was the last in and she too, jumped an immaculate clear to pull into the lead alongside the Germans.

As round two started, the youngest member of the German team entered the ring, and as the audience oohh'd and ahhh'd over every fence with her, she posted another clear to add to the zero German score.

Three ponies later and Georgie was on the edge of her seat as Davey entered the ring. He had produced Carlos from a novice and knew the pony inside out and, although it also was relatively inexperienced at this level, it had jumped really well in the team trials held across the country before the selection for Hagen.

To her delight, the pair put in a foot perfect round, inside the time. Now it was her turn to show what she was made of and prove she was a strong part of this British team.

In the collecting ring Allie felt perfect. Georgie could feel the controlled power underneath her as she soared over the practice fences. Called to the arena there was just time to tighten her girth and hear the 'good luck' messages from Gerald and Lorraine.

Trotting confidently forward she went straight to the judges box and saluted. Yet again she could feel the silence of the crowd as they waited to see what this new British combination could do. Coming round to the first Georgie became totally focused on the job in hand, shutting out any thought other than the route she was taking, the number of strides she was putting between each fence and getting through the finish.

Trusting her mount implicitly, she knew she was clear as she felt the mare stretch for the tape at the water. Sitting back and taking control she easily made the five strides to the planks, clearing them with room to spare. Coming round to the treble she followed team instructions completely and smiled as she knew she came to the fence on a perfect stride.

Through the finish, inside the time, and the second clear round for Britain. Jumping off in the collecting ring she couldn't wait to throw her arms round Allie's neck and get out the polos she'd remembered to put in her jacket pocket. "I love you so much Allie, that was just fantastic. You gave me such a fantastic ride. Thank you so much."

Lorraine and Gerald were quick to add their congratulations, and Lizzie took Allie away to walk her round and cool her off before returning her to the stables. There was an hour break between the two rounds, time for her to have the tack off, a rub down and relax.

Georgie took her place back in the stands, managing a quick wave to her mother across the arena. She was so happy and so proud. Job half done!

Once all the third team riders had completed their rounds only Germany and Great Britain had clean sheets. But Georgie knew the pressure was really on Sean now, as he needed to jump clear to stay in the running. The Germans already had three clears, but the fourth also jumped clear, making the home crowd roar their appreciation. As Sean entered the ring a balloon floated across the arena, spooking Magic and unsettling him. Sean calmly patted him on the neck, took his time doing a couple of small circles and a rein back, before confidently making his way to the first.

Still on edge Magic rubbed the first fence in front, but luckily it stayed in place. Another close call at the water, where both judges got up to look at the plastic tape, but fortunately neither raised a flag in the air. Coming to the planks Georgie could see Magic was pulling strongly, but Sean got him back just in time to clear them with ease. Only the combination to go, she thought, watching him jump the triple bar and a square oxer with inches to spare.

Following the team orders to the letter, she watched as Magic jumped the combination faultlessly, looking as though he had done it all his life. As they galloped through the finish she leapt to her feet and cheered. Another clear for Britain.

As the first rounds came to an end it was clear the competition was going to be between Britain and Germany, with both France and Holland close behind with just four faults apiece. Anything could happen.

Lorraine and Gerald gathered their team around

them. They explained how it was much easier to make mistakes in the second round. They had jumped clear, so they would all be a little more relaxed. The ponies knew their way around and would also be more relaxed. This was where they had to really concentrate. Britain needed three more clears - there was no room for mistakes.

After the pep talk the riders went across to the picnic area to have some snacks before the second round. Georgie wished she could go across and talk through the course with her mum, but the rules were very clear. She had to stay with the team and not get distracted in any way.

She found the German snacks unusual. As a lover of English sausages, she took an instant dislike to the Bratwurst and Blutworst that always seemed to be on offer. Fortunately, today there was cheese and bread, along with some bright red apples, so she managed to eat something before her nerves started getting to her again.

It seemed she'd only closed her eyes for a second before Lorraine was calling them all to get up and follow her across to the competitors stand where they would have a bird's eye view of the rounds to come.

Holding hands as they walked across, all feeling a strong team bond, she still really felt for Robbie who could take no further part in the competition because of his fall in the first round. He seemed to take it all in his stride she supposed because he was still likely, with his background, to make the European team regardless. She didn't have the same confidence.

The bell rang, giving the riders a five-minute warning, and Lorraine gave her final team briefing. "We can win this. We may only have three riders, so every score will count, but we have the best riders, the best ponies and we can do it. Believe in yourselves."

The three riders had to wait for all the first team riders to go before Davey and Carlos cantered into the ring. The first and second German and French riders had jumped a clear and then the second German rider had a pole down – but they had four riders so could afford to drop one of the rounds. Every rider now was getting rousing applause from the growing audience as the competition moved towards its climax.

Georgie could hardly bear to watch. Hearing the bell ring she sat on her hands to avoid feeling them shake. In under two minutes the round was over – another clear.

Tension was mounting and she felt enormous pressure. She knew the role of the third rider was crucial. She had to jump clear. There was no other choice. She knew Allie could do it, but could she? When she'd suffered the broken stirrup leather the day before she'd been heartbroken and thought she'd lost her chance. Well, against the odds, here it was again, and she wasn't going to mess it up.

Taking a minute to check her tack for a final, umpteenth, time and talking quietly to Allie, convinced she understood every word, she rode to the top of the shoot and waited for the rope to be lowered so she could walk into the ring.

Saluting to the judges box she ran over the course again in her mind, determined to take the same lines that proved so fruitful in the first round. Cantering through the start she felt Allie grow an inch underneath her, as though she too understood the importance of the job ahead of her.

For once the round went smoothly. Allie felt as though she'd grown wings, flying over the fences and not coming close to touching a pole. Putting her head down and ears flat to gallop through the finish, Georgie knew she'd done what she had set out to do – jump clear for her country.

With two clears recorded in the second round, it would be down to Sean and Magic to jump clear and either win outright or go into a jump off with the Germans, should they manage three clears.

The French rider went next, and had two fences down, dropping them down the order. Then a hush came over the arena as the last rider for the home team, the youngest girl taking part of Germany, calmy cantered into the ring.

Georgie had secretly admired this girl and her palomino pony. She showed no signs of nerves, despite her age, and rode very well, forward and accurate, hardly checking as she navigated the 12 fences. Galloping at the water Georgie could see she was going to have to take a long one and hoped the pony would clear the tape.

The judges were off their chairs as soon as she'd landed, examining where the front and back feet had landed. Suddenly there was a huge gasp from the crowd – and a muted 'yes' from the English team and supporters as a flag went up. The slightest of touches of a front hoof had marked the tape.

It took minutes for the crowd to realise the English team had won with a zero score and three riders. What an achievement. Again, Georgie felt for Robbie, but he was coming in for the presentation and she knew he'd have lots more opportunities to be part of winning teams in the future.

Their grooms were holding the four ponies in the collecting ring when the stewards came out with four navy blue rugs, one for each partnership, with the words Hagen Nations Cup winners embroidered on the sides. They were quite big for their mounts, but at this point no-one worried about such a small detail, they were just delighted to be the first into the ring, riding four abreast.

As they walked into the ring to rousing applause, Georgie felt every emotion surge through her young body. This was what she had worked so hard for, had left school for, being tutored at home, gone out and ridden in the rain, snow, soaring summer temperatures and even in thunderstorms.

As they reached the top of the ring, the rosettes and trophy were presented to the chef d'équipe and riders. Then silence as the live German band started to play the National Anthem, God Save the Queen.

She shut her eyes and felt the tears role down her cheeks. She was so proud. This was what the badge on her jacket meant and how it felt to represent, and win, for her country. She wanted time to stand still and to remember the feeling this gave her every minute of her life. Looking across to the collecting ring, she could see her mother and groom hugging one another and grabbing tissues from a box being passed around.

What a day. One she was never going to forget.

Chapter
9

Going Home

Going home in her mother's car the next morning, Georgie closed her eyes and thought about how far she'd come. From her first pony, the love of taking part in competitions, the ups and downs of both winning and losing... she was certain this was the career she wanted, however hard and difficult the road would be.

So far she'd been remarkably injury-free, but she knew there was a huge risk attached to this sport. Ponies weren't machines and could spook or stop at anything, even things at times only in their imaginations!

She remembered when, at 13 and just starting out on her 'professional' career, she'd pleaded with her parents to let her go hunting. She'd heard from her friends what fun this was and, having already ridden her sister's pony around a cross country course, she could think of nothing better to do on Boxing Day.

Plaiting Taspa up and making sure he started the day clean, she hacked to the local pub where the meet was. Seeing the hounds and sensing the palpable excitement around her, she felt Taspa getting more and more wound up, trotting on the spot and throwing the odd whinny before the horn sounded and they were off at a smart trot along the road.

Positioning herself in the middle of the pack, it wasn't long before they turned off on a wide track into Forestry Commission land. She knew her parents were following on foot, and wouldn't be able to keep up, so she concentrated on settling down to enjoy the day.

Heavy rain had made the going quite slippery, but Taspa was always steady on his feet, and cantering along the tracks listening to the hounds barking, she felt a new kind of freedom and began to understand why people loved this sport so much.

Deep into the woods, where trees met at the top enveloping them in semi-darkness, they came to a halt, letting the hounds pick up the scent. Then they were off again, at speed, as the huntsman kept them on the track and stopped. watching the hounds start off across a ploughed field to the side.

She hadn't thought much about the jumping she would do – not its height or width. Suddenly she saw the start of the field jumping off a bank, sliding to the bottom and hopping over a hedge into the plough.

Taspa, keen to join them, and certainly not willing to get left behind, took a huge leap down the bank, lost his footing at the bottom and fell to the ground, trapping Georgie's right leg underneath him. As she screamed in pain, he jumped up, standing on her leg with all his weight as he struggled to regain his balance.

Georgie knew she was hurt, but not how badly. Struggling to stand up she put her weight on her right leg and immediately crashed to the ground. Within minutes she was surrounded by other members of the field and told to lie still, an ambulance was on its way.

It seemed like hours before a plan was made but, in reality, it was minutes. The ambulance wouldn't be able to get to her, so a Land Rover was beating its way down the tracks and she'd be lifted into the back and moved into the ambulance already waiting on the main road.

Her parents were close to the ambulance and all they knew was that there'd been an accident. Filled with fear, they had an uncanny feeling that Georgie was hurt. And when they heard the faller was a palomino pony, they realized their fears were justified.

Georgie was experiencing tremendous pain, almost blacking out, and heard to her horror the paramedics saying they thought her leg was broken. Whisked off to Reading hospital and A&E, her parents sat with her in a cubicle waiting for the doctor to come, and then saw her wheeled off along a windowless and empty corridor for an Xray.

Waiting for news was awful. Her mother thought how lucky she was to only have a leg injury, her father was imagining all sorts of far worse scenarios, head injuries being top of his list. He'd always been terrified of something like this happening, one of the reasons he often chose to stay at home rather than travel to events.

Forty minutes later she was back. Her leg was broken in two places and needed plastering from the ankle to above the knee. Fortunately, the view was that with the support it would heal itself, no operation was needed. Georgie had seen other riders having to have plates and pins inserted so she was grateful that wasn't going to happen in her case.

Three hours later she was given some crutches and allowed to go home. The news hadn't been good, she wouldn't be able to ride for three months, and her next appointment was six weeks away. What would happen to her horses during this time?

She'd managed to qualify her hot skewbald mare, Azzie, for the prestigious Blue Chip Championships and knew it was going to be a struggle to get to the finals. But she had to challenge herself and was determined to do her best to make it. In the meantime, she'd ask a good friend of hers, Jayne, to take over the ride and keep her fit.

As the weeks passed, slowly, Georgie found herself getting more and more frustrated. She had learnt how to move around with her crutches and was spending more and more time out in the yard brushing and talking to her ponies. She was desperate to ride again and was hoping the first hospital appointment was going to give her all the all-clear.

The day of her long-awaited appointment dawned bright and sunny and she hoped that was a good omen. Waiting for another Xray she was certain the plaster would be coming off. She was putting weight on her leg now and could feel it growing in strength. She knew she had lost a lot of muscle tone but was sure she could soon get that back with some careful exercising.

But the doctor was not happy. While the bones were knitting, there was still more time needed, she must be patient, and the plaster would remain in place for a further six weeks. She was gutted. She'd been so hopeful and now she could see her chance of competing in the Blue Chip finals was disappearing into the sunset. Yes, there would be other years, but this was her and Azzie's year, she was certain of it.

Nothing could console her that evening, and she knew she had to make plans to do what was best for Azzie and to give her the best chance to shine. After several long telephone calls with Jayne and their two mums talking too, it was agreed Azzie would move to Jayne's yard for the next two months so they could become a true partnership. Hard though it was to let her go, Georgie knew in her heart it was the right decision. She would be a spectator, not a rider this time around.

In the fourth month, just before the finals, Georgie

had well and truly had enough. Without either of her parents knowing, she tacked up Misty, the JA pony she had on loan, used a chair to get on board, and set off down the quiet country lane outside their house with her right leg sticking out almost at right angles, with no stirrup attached.

This became a daily routine, her parents had no way of stopping her, such was her determination. She still smiles to the day about how puzzled the doctor was at her 12-week appointment to find the plaster rubbed down on the inside and, once removed, how she walked straight out of the consulting room without her crutches!

The day of Azzie's final was wet and cold. She saw Azzie rugged up in the collecting ring, tack gleaming below several heavy rugs, and was delighted when the mare gave a gently whinny of recognition as she walked towards her.

"Come on girl, this is your day," she said as she fed her a couple of her favourite polo mints. "You've got a jockey nearly as good as me, and you can win! Win it for me, please."

Over 40 ponies had qualified for the novice final, and Azzie had been drawn 36th to go, so Georgie knew she had a long wait. The arena was dressed beautifully, with fresh flowers everywhere, and the course was proving quite difficult and spooky for the amateur riders. By the time it was her turn, there were just seven clears.

Georgie was learning how it felt to watch a pony she had produced, and qualified, being ridden by someone else in a class she should have been contesting... and she was finding it hard. Very hard.

As Azzie entered the ring she felt the butterflies leaping around inside her stomach. She conquered the urge to shut her eyes and watched as her clever but difficult mare cleared the course. "Clear round number 8, and the fastest recorded" shouted out the announcer.

Hobbling down to the collecting ring she went through the jump off course with Jayne, giving her advice where she could, believing her mare would win if she took the shortest routes and kept all the poles in their flat cups. She was naturally fast if you had the confidence to let her go forward and Jayne had the invaluable experience.

Last to go – because she had posted the fastest first round of the now 10 clears – a hush covered the large crowd packing the stands. "And now our last to go, number 54, Just Two Tone ridden by Jayne Livingstone for owner Georgie Stones."

Azzie threw in a buck as she approached the start and Jayne struggled to get her on the right stride to the first. She hit it, hard, but the pole bounced back into the cups. Cutting inside to the double she was ahead on the clock, and decided not to risk the turn at the top of the arena, inside a curved wall. Seeing a gallop to the last, a vertical, she took a pull to get her back on her hocks, and they cleared the fence with ease. But, glancing up at the clock, she saw that last pull had cost her dear and she went into second place by 2/100ths of a second. So close, just a whisker between first and second.

The crowd cheered and Georgie fought her way down to the collecting ring. "Well done Jayne, you rode brilliantly, I'm so pleased," she said. Jayne replied that she felt she'd let her down and should have trusted Azzie enough and not taken that last pull.

"I've always been taught to gallop at an oxer, but take a pull for a vertical," Georgie said. "You did the right thing. If you'd kept going you might have had it down and ended up 8th or 9th rather than 2nd."

As the ponies came in the for prize giving, Georgie had been surprised to hear her name called out.

The judges had heard about her hunting accident and broken leg and thought it right and proper that she should go into the ring for the presentation.

To her surprise an Olympic rider, one of her heros, was there to hand out the rosettes and he made a special effort to congratulate her and wish her well in the sport – a pick me up that stayed with her a long time. Years later she was to jump against the same rider in a World Cup qualifier in Millstreet in Ireland and share equal 8th place with him, qualifying for the final.

She never forgot his kind and encouraging words that day and a picture of her, next to him, holding the second place rosette, held pride of place on her dressing table for many years.

Chapter
10
Ariving Home

Sitting in the lounge on the ferry crossing the Channel, Georgie smiled to herself as she remembered those early days with Azzie. Yes, it had been hard sitting that final out, but she knew now that she had much bigger things to come. She'd since qualified Azzie for the Junior Newcomers final at Horse of the Year Show, so had that to look forward to in the autumn.

She and Allie were going to have the rest of the week off before planning their diary for the next three months in the run up to the European Championships. The County Show circuit was up and running and there were often pony Grand Prixs on the schedule. There was also a list of six European pony trials, from which the successful team would be selected, and her aim was to compete in each.

The final two trials were on consecutive days at the Royal Show at Stoneleigh in Warwickshire. And, after the second day, the team would be announced.

Was she confident she would be selected? No, she

wasn't, she still had that fear that something was going to go wrong. She could have another tack disaster, the pony could go lame, she could have another accident, a better pony and rider combination could appear in the three long months ahead... but she would give it her best shot.

She had a great support team around her, and while she couldn't wrap Allie up in cotton wool, she would do all she could to keep her safe and sound.

At the time she could never have known how close she came to disaster.

Allie had never tried to jump out of the post and rail paddocks at home and seemed happy turned out on her own, or with her best pony friend, Tina, or My Lady Blue, who Georgie's mum had bought from Ireland. Tina was another 'hot' pony who she had raved to her trainer about in the early days, really believing at the time she was a better performer than Allie.

Having been kept in for a few days as heavy rain had made the paddock muddy and slippery, her groom had turned both ponies out together this particular morning, without rugs, to let them enjoy some early summer sunshine on their backs. Allie was having a two-week break between shows and was enjoying the down time.

Her father was busy in the vegetable plot adjoining the house when he heard an unusual loud crack, like a shot from a gun. Puzzled he went round to the yard in time to see both ponies galloping up the field towards the metal five-bar gate.

To his horror he saw Tina trailing one of her back legs behind her, only using three legs to keep up with Allie.

Calling for immediate help, Georgie, her mother and groom ran to the field and immediately realized Tina's back off-hind was damaged, looking as though it was broken.

As she tried to stand on three legs, she kept losing her balance and it was all two of them could do to keep her upright. How she had got up the field in a gallop was hard to imagine.

"Quick, call the vet, get him here as quickly as possible," shouted her Dad as Georgie ran into the house, fighting back tears. She knew instinctively this was going to be a very bad situation.

Putting Allie back into safety, in her stable, they all talked quietly to Tina, stroked her, calmed her and tried to keep her still. It was clear she was in considerable pain, and while there was no blood or visible cut, her leg was very definitely in two parts, looking a lot worse than Georgie's had when she had suffered the same fate.

Within 30 minutes Justin, the vet they had used throughout their pony lives, swept into the drive. He had broken every speed limit to get there as quickly as he could and, what he was to do next, was to give Tina every chance of recovery.

The first decision was to get her to Liphook Animal Hospital, about an hour's drive away, where their chief surgeon, John, would Xray the leg and make an honest assessment on whether it was worth operating or not.

To give her the best chance of arriving literally in one piece, Justin, with everyone's help, proceeded to bandage, splint and secure her hind leg. Once that was complete the lorry was carefully backed as close as possible to where she was patiently standing, the ramp lowered, and step by step she was lifted on to the back. This whole process took nearly two hours, as no-one could risk her trying to put more weight on her broken leg.

Lizzie the groom got in the back with her to try and steady her and Georgie's mum drove the lorry as slowly as she dared, taking particular care not to unbalance Tina in the back.

Georgie had long given up trying to fight back the tears that rolled continually down her cheeks. For so long this pony had been her number one, the one she had loved from the moment she arrived from Ireland. The one she had jumped her first Paul Fabs with and the one that had won so many speed classes. She was also aware this was probably the pony that had catapulted her into the limelight and had given her the opportunity to be considered as Allie's rider. Only a week earlier she had refused a substantial offer for her, preferring to keep her as her second pony.

They'd had so many firsts together. When there was an invitation for some British riders to travel to Megeve, a ski resort in the French Alps in the Mont Blanc massif, Tina and Georgie got one of the 'golden tickets.'

As a family they'd driven to the resort and stayed in the Four Seasons Hotel. The cobbled streets were hard to see with feet of snow making walking around hard, and she remembered how worried she'd been to jump on the compacted snow and ice. She had seen polo played on snow, but never heard of horses jumping on it.

It had been deemed far too risky to travel Allie, so Tina got the invitation and, as she was being tacked up for the first time, with massive three-inch studs being screwed into her shoes to give her extra grip, Georgie wondered if it would feel any different.

Unfortunately, in the second competition, Tina had struck into herself with one of the large studs opening quite a large wound on her near fore. Georgie could remember how the blood stained the white, white snow and filled her with concern that the wound was a lot worse than it was. Sadly, this put an end to the jumping, but there was still a spa to enjoy and a chance to ski.

She could remember how cross the chef d'equip had got with her sister Vikki who, when at the top of the mountain, she'd fallen over as she tried to get off the ski lift elegantly, and then looked at the village far below, lights twinkling in the early evening, and announced there was no way she could 'ski down there'.

Georgie knew she could make it, carefully working out stop points on the way, planning her journey down into separate little boxes. Her sister could only see one way down – and that was one, solid, run.

After a lot of argument, they both got to the bottom safely, went back to the hotel and got ready for dinner. They were all going out for a meal that night and a well-known sponsor of British Showjumping over the years, his wife and children, were joining the party.

Negotiating the icy pavements that evening, her mother was the first to lose her footing and go flying across the path, landing unceremoniously in a pile of thick snow.

Next down was John, the sponsor and, when he scrambled to his feet, he discovered that his highly valuable cygnet ring, always worn on this fourth finger, had come off and was nowhere to be seen.

Six people started shamelessly searching for the chunky gold ring that had a diamond set in its centre. Scrabbling around in the dark, pushing snow aside, certain it couldn't have gone far, but getting more concerned by the minute. After nearly an hour of searching, and everyone getting colder as every minute passed, his wife Anne suddenly shouted 'got it'.

Remarkably it had flown over the top of a nearby snowdrift and fallen right next to a drain. A couple more inches and it would have been gone forever.

Sliding the ring back on his finger, the mood changed to one of happy laughter, as the group headed to the chosen restaurant for the night. Cold and damp, they were all delighted to be seated next to roaring log fire inside the chalet-style restaurant.

She also remembered that first Paul Fabs competition at South View and how she'd jumped the biggest course in her life on Tina that day. South View always built up to height and she considered it beginners' luck when she posted the first clear.

When she'd walked the course, she was shocked by how big the track was, particularly towards the end, and had to keep reminding herself that riding it would be just the same as riding a 1m or 1m20 course at home.

Tina had flown round the course that day, not touching a pole and, as the competition had been early in the New Year and a lot of combinations were just starting out on their Paul Fabs journey for the year, there were only three clear rounds. She remembered the feeling this gave her – to be one of the best three of the weekend.

For the jump off she'd thrown caution to the wind. It seemed every fence had gone up at least one hole, and it looked bigger than ever. She turned tight and kept her rhythm going but, unfortunately, had the vertical coming out of the combination down in front.

"Never mind girl, that was a great introduction to this level," she said, patting her pony and giving her some polos she'd stored in her jacket pocket. When the winning announcement was made, they'd taken second place, and were now second on the Paul Fabs leaderboard, a competition that ran through the first four months of every year and was run as a 'league'.

Now, as the lorry was travelling slowly to the veterinary hospital, she was keeping everything crossed that Tina would make it. But she knew the odds were against it.

Leaving the unloading to the professionals, Georgie and her mum went into the waiting room. After what seemed like hours, John came out to talk to them.

"The good news is that Justin has done an amazing job," he said. "By bandaging and splinting the leg as he has, she has the best chance. We are just doing some Xrays and I'll be back shortly once I've had a chance to look at them. At the moment we don't know how bad this break is."

They sat quietly together waiting for more news. Eventually Georgie spoke up. "Mum if they can't give us back a pony that can happily walk around the field and graze, I feel it will be best to have her put to sleep. I don't know how I will cope with that, but I couldn't bear to see her hobbling around when I know how much she loved her competition work and her hacking." Her mother silently agreed with her and was a little surprised Georgie had spoken those words.

Within the hour John was back in the waiting room. "Her leg is badly broken in two places," he said, flashing the Xray up on a screen against the wall. "Look, you can see the clear breaks in her cannon bone." Georgie jumped up to look and could very clearly see the two breaks he was referring to.

"The good news is that we can mend them. Technology has moved forwards considerably. But this will be the worst break we've tried to repair, so I can't promise to give you a pony you will be able to ride – ever again."

He went on to explain that they would open the leg and insert a long titanium plate, the sort used in skiing accidents, held in place by 20 titanium screws. She would be plastered for six weeks, and the plate and screws would remain in place for her lifetime, giving her more strength in that leg.

So much was going to depend on her temperament, as she would remain at the hospital for up to three months, and for the first eight or more weeks would be tied up, preventing her from moving around or even from lying down.

"If she comes through this, she'll be able to return home, but will have to be stabled. A bit later she'll be able to go out to grass, being held on a lunge line, two or three times a day. At no point for the next nine or so months must she trot or canter. No extra pressure on that leg. It must be given the best opportunity to heal."

Georgie thought there were a lot of 'if's' in what John was telling her and said she needed time to talk to her mum. John left them alone to talk, and Georgie was determined to do her best for her pony.

"I've been thinking we could put her in foal once she had got through this," she said. "Tina is a full-up 14.2hh pony, so if we used AI and a bigger show jumping stallion, maybe we could breed something I could take into the horse classes in the future."

Georgie rang her father to give him an update and he was happy they had a possible plan. Tina had always been one of his favourites, she had been so easy to look after on occasions she had been left at home. "I'll support whatever decision you make Georgie, it's your decision alone to make."

She went out to have some fresh air and came back mind made up. Waiting for John to return she said: "We'll go ahead with the operation John, do the best to keep her quiet and under your care and look to breed from her next Spring. She deserves her chance."

Secretly John was happy they had chosen this route. He knew that if he was able to use this as a case study, and share the operation with other equine vets, his hospital would get more referrals and gain in notoriety, for the right reasons.

Decision made, Tina went into surgery. They went home, knowing it could be many hours before an update. The first news would let them know whether or not she had made it through the operation and how successful it had been.

Some four hours later the home phone rang. John reported that Tina was coming round from the op, the metal plate had been successfully screwed into place, and that the next few days would be critical.

She didn't know it at the time, but it was to be a long, and educational, 15 months before Tina was confirmed in foal to a lovely dark chestnut stallion that had jumped on Nations Cups with its rider, a top lady in the sport.

The foal had been born in the middle of the night, was also chestnut, and named 'Lucky'. Tina was a great mother, she really loved her foal and Georgie was always going to be so happy to see them grazing together, always gently nuzzling each other, as if to confirm they were both there, and happy. Tina was never ridden again, but she did prove to be a very successful brood mare, and eventually found a great pet and companion home on the Welsh hills.

Chapter

11

A Long Summer

Remembering those days, which now seemed so long ago, Georgie thought how lucky she was that it had been Tina that broke her leg that day, not Allie. She felt guilty even thinking that but realised that was how it was. To this day no-one in the family had been able to work out how the accident had occurred and it seemed a strange twist of fate that when the two ponies were side by side, it had been Tina that, for some reason, had been the one injured.

Next up on the spring calendar were some more Paul Fabs qualifiers, that moved from equestrian centre to equestrian centre, around the country, and then a move into the summer schedule of European pony trials before the final team selection that July.

The Winter League had been decided before Hagen and played a big role in selecting the team that had travelled. Although they had only contested six of the 10 qualifiers on offer, they'd topped the table and were well ahead, on points, of the nearest rider in second place. Her instructions throughout had been to jump double clears each time, not to take Allie against the clock, and she had followed them to the letter, notching up six double clears.

Two of her favourite competition venues were Bicton arena and Wales and the West, and some bigger competitions had been ignored so Georgie could travel there with her team of ponies. It was important to her to produce ponies to sell on to other up and coming riders as well as to have fun in some of the less professional events.

Bicton was run by the South West Show Jumping Club and boasted a fantastic all-grass course in the main arena, a bit like an amphitheatre, with seating overlooking the Derby-style course.

It was based in Devon linked to Bicton Agricultural College, and to get there the lorry had to be driven down narrow country lanes which always concerned her mother and the groom who sometimes drove. Overhanging branches put scratches in the paintwork, and there were many 'near misses' as speeding motorists were not expecting to find big lorries on their local lanes.

In the early days of competition her mum had bought an old Bedford lorry with lots of wood encasing the back and had arranged to pick it up at Bicton. She had driven it around the showground empty to get used to it, and then moved all their gear into it ready for the drive home. Loading the ponies was quite straightforward, they soon settled into the new lorry.

As she drove away from the showground there was a huge crash from the living area and the sound of breaking glass and crockery. Her mum had completely forgotten that loose items had to be put away or 'nailed down' and had left the lunch crockery and cutlery on the work surfaces to crash to the floor. There wasn't much of it left now!

As you leave the showground there's a really steep hill to navigate. It wasn't long before there was a long queue of traffic behind them and her mum started to panic. The lorry was struggling to make it up the hill – what had she bought? Crashing a gear she ground to a halt, the lorry stalling. Frightened of doing her first hill start, she got Georgie to get out of the passenger seat, go behind the lorry, and wave the queue of cars passed. She refused to set off again until there were no cars behind her, worrying the lorry would roll backwards into the one first in the line.

That aside, Bicton was an extremely popular show and venue. You had to be quick with your bookings, or you wouldn't get into the right classes.

Georgie's mum had booked a local farm cottage to stay in for the week, and was sharing it with her father, who had been so instrumental in buying Allie.

The cottage was a short walk down the road. Georgie and her groom would be sharing the horsebox. It was great to be based on the ground itself as families knew each other well and there were frequent BBQs where groups would get together in the evening and talk about the day's activities. There was also a big open barn where meals would be served throughout the day and sometimes entertainment would be put on in the evenings...karaoke was one of the most popular nights.

During the day, if you were a class sponsor, you were given an invitation to the sponsor's lounge. This was a lovely warm pavilion overlooking the main arena and Georgie loved the fact she could take her grandfather there and leave him warm and comfortable while she competed. He'd become very popular with the show organisers and they always made certain he had plenty of his favourite tea to hand. Great food, prepared by the organisers themselves, was on offer throughout the day – a favourite was the typical Devon cream tea.

This particular show Georgie had taken three ponies, Allie for the open classes in the main arena, a relatively new ride, Libbie, for the lower level of opens, and Azzie, her favourite skewbald novice.

On the first day she had won all three classes she had entered, much to the delight of her grandfather. That night they had taken off in the car and gone down to the pebble beach in Budleigh Salterton and eaten fish and chips, covered in salt and vinegar, on the beach front, watching the sky turn bright red as the sun set.

The second day dawned bright and sunny and again

Allie won her class in the main arena, with a time 5 seconds faster than her nearest rival. When it came to the prize giving, they invited her grandfather into the ring and, as he stood proudly next to his granddaughter, he was thinking how proud Beryl, his dearly departed wife, would have been at this moment.

Due to the high number of entries in some of the other classes, being held in other nearby rings, her second open class that she was to contest with Libbie, was also being held in the main arena.

She seemed to like riding 'hot' mares, and Libbie was no exception to this. She'd been bought from a leading boy rider based near Harrogate and Georgie had loved the feel the mare gave her as the fences got bigger. She'd won the National JC Championships just before purchase and she was certain she would go a long way.

Entering the main ring she was feeling confident. Libbie had never jumped in this arena before, but that didn't stop her from wanting to win.

Some of the fences were rustic, the sort you would normally come across our hunting or on a Derby course, but Libbie had never spooked and Georgie had no reason to think she might.

At the far end of the arena was a double of water trays. There is a much bigger famous pair of these in the Hickstead Derby. As she cantered into the ring, she took her pony down to these and cantered past them, making sure she had a good look at them before she came towards them to jump.

The water trays were 6A and 6B, so quite early on the course. As she came round the corner to jump them, she could feel the pony underneath her back off. Giving her a good kick in the ribs, and a slight snack down her neck, she was confident the pony would jump.

To her surprise Libbie threw in a very determined, and quick, stop, bringing her whole body to a grinding halt and dropping her head and shoulder at the same time. Not being able to stop falling off and landing hard and unceremoniously on the ground, she slid forwards into the water tray and, as well as banging her head hard on the pole got soaked by the blue dye in the bottom of the tray which quickly covered her white breeches.

One of the fence judges ran across and told her to lie still. Her groom ran in and caught Libbie who was, by now, enjoying a good graze of the lush long grass. Georgie felt fine, and wanted to get up, but was prevented from doing so while the St John Ambulance team were scrambled and moved across the ring.

Gently her hat was removed and Georgie found herself being moved on to a stretcher that was used to carry her up to the First Aid room on site. Joined by her concerned mother and grandfather she found herself going through several tests before she was allowed to sit up.

It was a hard and fast rule that any rider who had suffered any kind of head injury had to be checked out by the local hospital. Georgie was trying to convince everyone she was fine and had no need to go to hospital, when she heard the siren of the local ambulance announcing its arrival outside.

Her demands to be allowed to go back and ride were ignored. Forced to get into the ambulance for the short ride to Budleigh Salterton hospital, she lay back on the stretcher and gave in.

The paramedics carried out a whole range of checks, took her blood pressure, and put something resembling a clothes peg on the end of her index finger. This was linked to a machine that recorded her heartbeat, and there was something comforting in hearing its steady 'beep beep'.

The ground was rough as they left the showground, and suddenly the 'beep beep' stopped. There was only silence. Georgie shot upright and said: 'my heart's stopped, am I dead?' much to the amusement of the ambulance team. Going over the bumps had dislodged the clothes peg linking her to the machine, so of course the 'beeping' was silenced...

After a thorough check over in the hospital she was allowed to return to the showground, with a strict instruction not to ride before the following day. And not to ride at all if she had a headache or felt dizzy.

That evening Georgie, her mum, grandfather and

groom went to join two other families for a BBQ. The bbq was run on a 'bring and cook' basis. The host supplied the salads and bread but would get others to bring their own meat to kept costs down. It also allowed the participants to eat what they fancied.

There was much laughter as Alex, her grandfather, told some of his war stories and the tale of when he had driven across Europe with Georgie when she was a baby. A Volkswagen camper van had taken them from Hampshire to Venice and leaving the sleeping accommodation in the van to her and her parents, he'd pitched a tent each night next to the vehicle.

On the first night driving through eastern France it had been dark when they arrived on the campsite. All had lent a hand pitching the tent and Georgie's mum had woken up to heavy rain hitting the roof and making a series of resounding bangs during the night. She soon dropped back to sleep and didn't think any more of it until daylight, when it was easy to see the tent had been pitched at the bottom of a hill, and the heavy rain had forged a wide gully leading from the top, straight underneath Alex's tent.

When he came out of the zipped opening a few minutes later, everything he had in the tent was soaking wet. How he had stayed there overnight was a miracle. It took days before his clothes and bedding dried out.

Then there was the time when, one evening, they

went to a small Italian restaurant on the shores of Lake Garda. The menu was all in Italian, and no-one had any idea what they were ordering. Choosing a starter and a main course, they were all amazed when the same dish turned up for both courses. Macaroni cheese. The only change was the addition of ham in the main course version.

Getting off to bed about 10pm, with a bit of a headache, Georgie slept soundly, dreams of winning the Grand Prix the following day rolling around inside her head.

Sunday dawned cloudy and windy. There'd been some light rain overnight, and the ground was soft. She was glad she'd been drawn early in the class so she wasn't covering ground churned up by previous ponies.

The Grand Prix was the biggest class of the weekend and, with a £250 first prize, it had attracted a lot of entries, with some people travelling to the show just for this one class.

Looking at the entries she noticed three potential team members on the start list and knew the class was going to be hard to win, especially from the front. She'd been drawn 5th to go and knew the order would remain the same if she got through to the jump off.

As usual she walked the course twice, taking the uphill and downhill gradients into account and noticing the course builder, 'Bob the builder', was the same person building for the European trials, and that he'd had asked some big questions. There were two doubles instead of a combination, the first a double of verticals, the second a wide oxer in and two strides to a big vertical with light poles on very flat cups.

There were wavy planks, a new bicycle fence she hadn't seen before, a solid spotted wall and a big triple bar which, although it looked huge, she knew would ride well.

There was also an unusual addition, a table, normally included in a derby course. It consisted of a vertical jump up on to a flat grassy bank, four strides across the top, then a vertical drop down back on to the normal arena surface. Georgie had never jumped one of these but didn't see it as a problem.

As they started to warm up in the collecting ring, she saw just how hard the class was. Two riders had retired, one had had eight faults and, just as she was entering the ring, the fourth had 20. She knew they weren't the top combinations, but even so they were clearly finding the course hard.

Saluting to the judge's box she made her way across the arena to the table to let Allie take a look at it. She didn't seem bothered in the least so, cantering a circle before she went through the timing, she was soon on her way.

To her surprise, as she came round to the table, she felt her mare back off, but knew her well enough by now to give her a sharp dig in the ribs to move her forwards off her leg. She jumped onto the top, cantered across the middle and hopped off as if she had done it all her life.

The first clear round. She couldn't be happier. With another 42 pony combinations to jump, she had a long wait before the jump off, and was surprised when more clear rounds came towards the end of the class. At the halfway point there were only two clears but, by the end, there were a total of seven partnerships to go against the clock.

By now parts of the course were quite ploughed up, as it had been drizzling solidly most of the morning, and Georgie knew she would have to take some of the sharp turns carefully. The last thing she wanted was for Allie to turn up tight, lose her footing and fall.

It's never easy to go first in a jump off. Do you go all out to win and risk having a fence? Or do you try to jump a clear round and not worry about the time? Or is it a combination of the two, as fast as you dare, but safe?

She'd decided to go for it. She wanted to win and wanted to have the red, white and blue sash placed across her body. There was also a wreath to go round the winning pony's neck and she'd never won one of those before. This time she wasn't under any team orders and felt the opportunity to win was hers.

Taking all the risks she dared, Allie jumped clear again, this time taking out strides and jumping across fences to get in the tight turns. There was a huge round of applause as she galloped through the finish and posted a clear in a time of 32.06 seconds.

Now came the wait. The second and third riders tried to beat her time and both had fences. The fourth rider was her old rival, Davey, on his potential European ride, Carlos. Georgie could hardly bear to watch and gave a huge sigh of relief when he jumped clear but missed her time by two seconds.

The fifth contender turned too sharp to the wall and, as Georgie had feared, lost his footing, his hind legs slid away, and the rider managed, miraculously, to stay on board and finish the course, some way off the time.

With just one rider to go, she got back on Allie and started walking around the collecting ring. The prize was so close to being hers, she could see the wreath around Allie's neck. The last to go was a local rider she didn't know well, and she wondered what decision she would make – try and beat Georgie and still jump double clear, or forget the time, go double clear and end up in third place, taking home some good prize money?

After the first couple of fences, it was obvious she was going for the double clear. And that's exactly what she achieved, stopping the clock at exactly 38 seconds to finish third.

The steward came up to Georgie, asked her to dismount while they fitted a bright red wool rug over the pony's back, then put the sash over her shoulder and across her chest. The wreath and cup would be given to her in the ring.

To her surprise she saw the local paper was there to record her win, the photographer already in the ring snapping away, and that a former Olympian, who'd become a household name when the BBC used to cover the Horse of the Year Show live every night, was there to hand over the prize. She knew this was a big win, but hadn't realised it was this big.

Walking calmly into the ring she positioned Allie between the two potted trees that had been placed in the middle. She waited for her grandfather to join her before accepting the silver trophy and moving back on the saddle so a member of the arena party could fasten the wreath around Allie's neck.

Presentation done, she led the top 10 riders around the ring in a canter, to the booming Horse of the Year show music, always used in situations such as these, before the other nine peeled off and went into the collecting ring. Allie loved these moments, lived for them and, as they went around the ring in a flat-out gallop and approached the grandstand, she threw her huge rosette into the crowd for some future young champion to cherish.

What a show this had been. She'd long forgotten the fall from Libbie the previous day and, in fact, earlier on Sunday had jumped double clear on her in the Junior

Foxhunter competition completing the four double clears she needed to qualify for the second rounds.

Azzie, although still competing in smaller classes, had jumped double clear every day, and won enough prize money to cover most of her costs. This was an expensive sport, but with Allie's big win this afternoon, Georgie was certain that for once they had come home in profit.

Her grandfather was at the lorry by the time she got back, bursting with pride. He could see what the win had meant to his granddaughter and was so pleased he'd taken the gamble and agreed to buy the pony in memory of his wife. Georgie jumped off, went over to him, handing out a big hug before handing him the sash and wreath she had so wanted to win.

"This is for you grandad. If it wasn't for you, I wouldn't be following my dream. Take them home and put them up on the wall so you can remember this day forever. It's just the start of what we'll win in the next year or so, but this is the first big win here and I want you to keep them."

Feeling his eyes begin to water, Alex wondered what he'd done to have such an understanding and modest grandchild. He was looking forward to the rest of the season... and to the Europeans, now just three months away.

Chapter
12

The Summer Campaign

When the team got back from Bicton it was time for Alex to return to his home on the Isle of Wight and time for the ponies to have a week off, enjoying the early summer sun in their grassy paddocks.

Georgie and her trainer William sat down to plan the summer campaign, which would take in the team trials leading up to the Europeans, making sure some smaller classes were on the agenda to keep her pony sweet. There were also the second rounds to contest with both Libbie and Azzie, Libbie in the bigger Foxhunter and Azzie in the Newcomers. It was going to be a busy time.

Up to now the home stables had all been built by Georgie's father, inside a sound barn. They weren't the expensive American barn type; they were put together using his carpentry skills and had stood the test of time well.

Now a decision had been made to build a new block of five stables, including a corner foaling box, and the family were going through the rigours of applying, and eventually winning, planning permission to erect them. The plan was for them to be up and ready before the weather started to change in the autumn.

Georgie also had an intensive six weeks of studying to fit in around her riding as she was taking her GCSE's a year early as she was being home-schooled.

The home schooling hadn't been her parents preferred option. Along with her sister Vikki, she had been attending a local private school, St Nicholas, for girls only at the time and had been doing well in her academic work. She had lots of non-horsey friends there and always made time for them, enjoying shopping trips in the town centre and weekend trips to the beach or to one another's houses when she wasn't out competing.

As the number of ponies in her care had started to increase, Georgie had found it harder and harder to exercise them adequately. While the groom could lunge them, she didn't ride them or school them. When Allie joined the team it was clear show jumping was going to play an even bigger role in her life.

Her parents had paid a visit to the head teacher to explain. They talked about the time needed to work the ponies so they were all fit and ready to compete and the fact that Georgie was fast moving up to the top level of the pony showjumping ranks. They took with them her British Showjumping records which showed how successful she was being and how often she was competing.

They asked for her to be able to leave school early every afternoon. From 2.30pm, every day, there was a 90-minute sports period when either tennis or netball in the summer, or hockey and gym in the winter, would occur.

This would give their daughter an extra 90 minutes to work on the ponies and, more importantly, this could be done in the light, in the afternoon. Planning permission for lights around an arena was always hard to get and several times their application had been refused because it was close to a main country road.

They left that first meeting in shock. The headmistress had refused to even consider their request. She was adamant that Georgie had to stay in school and participate in what she described as a 'team sport'. The harder they argued, the more negative she became.

"But Georgie is taking place in team sports," Jane said. "She's been chosen to be in a team of five riders who're travelling to shows across the UK and Europe jumping to represent their country. Surely that's the highest level of team sport?"

But this lady was not for moving. Tapping her husband on the arm, Jane said "let's go, we're getting nowhere here, there's a longer fight ahead."

As they drove home, they worked out a plan. They

would write a formal letter to the board of governors, explaining the situation in full and, if that didn't work, they would go to the local paper with their story.

Jane was confident they'd win and knew that had the sport of rugby or football been featured in a private boys school, the child involved would have been encouraged and supported to spend more time in the sport. In addition, the school would have been proud of his achievements.

After the letter was posted, six weeks passed before there was a reply. The board of governors had supported the headmistress in her decision and Georgie would not be allowed to miss out on the daily sporting activity.

Fortunately, Jane had a good relationship with the local paper's editor, Alan Franklin, and rang him up with the news. He arranged for a reporter and photographer to visit at the weekend, interviewing both Georgie and her parents. The result was a whole front page devoted to the story in The Star the following week. If anything, this article seemed to make the school even more determined to stick to their guns.

Making a family decision, they decided that Georgie would leave St Nicks and be home schooled from the start of the next term. Her parents had already been searching for potential tutors and found one candidate who could teach English Language, English Literature and Maths, and a second tutor for French and Science.

They would try to get her six GCSE's all at a good grade, so her options later on were still available.

The home schooling had worked extremely well and Georgie had studied hard, mainly in the evenings once her ponies had been 'put to bed'. It had also meant that she was able to travel to three-day shows a lot more easily, taking prep with her and working in the lorry in between classes.

Now she had to face a tough revision time for all the subjects as exam dates were fixed and she would be travelling to a local examination centre to take the GSCEs in the coming weeks. Studying didn't always come easily, but she did believe her parents when they impressed on her how important it was to have a good grounding in the basic subjects.

Planning the summer campaign, Georgie could see she was only going to have three free weekends in the months ahead. This didn't worry her at all, she knew how committed she had to be to the sport to reach her dream of being selected to ride at the Europeans.

The next outing was to be to Church Farm in Staffordshire, an arena Georgie loved. It was a single ring with a warm-up, all grass, and was known for running regular pony events. The going was always good as the ground was well drained, and there was always a good selection of fences, including an open water jump and derby fences which wouldn't feature in the team trial.

All the top contenders for European places would be there. Once again she was back under 'team' orders and had been told by the Chef d'Equipe to try to jump a double clear, not to win the class. For the team, the selectors were looking for combinations that, as in Hagen, could jump clear rounds and put Britain first.

A warm-up class on the first day was set lower than she knew the trial itself would be, but it did include the open water, which she knew would be a question for some of the less experienced riders. She jumped round carefully, giving Allie plenty of time to take in the big arena and find her way, and jumped clear, inside the time, notching up a third place. So far so good.

That evening the competitive parents sat together watching one of the smaller pony classes from the edge of the bank. Although they were all keen for their children to do well the following day, they were friends, and tried to keep their negative thoughts to themselves. Somehow it didn't feel right to wish one of your competitors to have a fence down but, in reality, they did. They were certainly every bit as competitive as the Pony Club parents who were always known for stabbing one another in the back, given any opportunity.

The dads would often get together and leave the showground to walk to the local pub, the Fox and Hounds and, on this particular evening, it seemed there'd been a huge argument over which pony was the best.

Georgie's father was never involved, as he stayed at home to look after the ponies not travelling and the rest of the animals they kept on their smallholding – dogs, chicken, pigs and turkeys in the run up to Christmas.

Three fathers had got into the argument and, as the drink flowed, so did their determination to win the argument. The three ponies in question were a skewbald gelding, Serphant; a cremello gelding called Viscount and a chestnut gelding called Evergreen. All three were to end up on the shortlist and had previous records from the Europeans, the argument was really about which rider, and which pony, was the best.

Staggering back to the showground once time had been called, the owner of Evergreen slipped and fell into a ditch by the side of the road. The other two hardly noticed and continued back, vowing to continue their discussion in the morning.

Everyone in Evergreen's lorry was fast asleep and it wasn't until they woke up the following morning they realised David was missing. Waking up the Chef d'Equipe, and the other parents, they sent out a search party, horrified when they found David still asleep in the ditch where he'd collapsed the previous evening. Getting him back to the lorry and freshened up was the first job, then there was a team talk from the Chef d'Equipe, who certainly didn't mince her words.

"I can't tell you how disgusted I am by your behaviour last night," she said. "You're supposed to be setting an example for your children, instead you go out and get drunk and start an argument. I dread to think what would have happened if we'd been abroad and you'd got into an argument with some of the other teams' parents about the quality of their ponies. This is just how we do NOT behave.

"You're all adults, or at least I think you are, so I can hardly punish you. But I can tell you that your behaviour will be taken into account at selection time. I can't afford to take people on a team whose parents don't set an example. This has thrown a big cloud over the weekend and I'll be reporting the incident to the other selectors."

Although not directly involved, Davey and Georgie had also attended the meeting, as well as some of the other riders. The mood was sombre as the class got underway and Georgie went to talk to Sonja, Evergreen's rider, as she could see how upset she was.

"Please don't let this upset you Sonja," she said. "You know our chef can be quite tough. It was silly but obviously they got drunk and got into a fight. I'm sure it won't happen again and I don't think it'll have any effect on your selection. Just get out there today, forget everything, and concentrate on getting a clear."

Sonja thanked her and said she was so fed up with her father. It wasn't the first time he had got drunk at a show and, more than anything, she was embarrassed by his behaviour in front of her friends.

In no time at all it was time to walk the course and Georgie's trainer William had travelled up from his Gatwick base to give her tips on the distances and route to take. Putting the morning behind her, she tried to concentrate while he told her where she could make some time and where she should add, rather than remove, strides.

They sat down together to watch the start of the class. In the first 10 riders to go there was just one clear. The course hadn't seemed that difficult when it was walked and no one fence was causing the problem. Fences were falling all over the course.

The water jump, which now had a small white picket fence in front of it, had caused quite a few refusals but, apart from that, the faults had occurred evenly around the course.

Georgie really valued his advice. She knew he'd produced horses to the top level and felt lucky he'd agreed to coach her. In the next 12 months they were going to be travelling around Europe looking for horses that would move her career on into Juniors and Young riders but, right now, all his efforts were going on getting her to the Europeans.

With a few final words of encouragement, she found herself cantering into the ring, saluting and running over the course again in her head. When the bell rang she was ready to canter through the start.

She was confident that Allie would jump a clear and she did, well inside the time, thanks to the turn inside the triple bar to the double of oxers. The time was always tighter under FEI rules than British Showjumping rules but, if you kept moving forwards, rather than adding strides, you were usually OK.

When all had jumped the first round, Georgie was pleased to see six of them had gone into the jump off, including Sonja, who clearly hadn't been distracted by the morning's activity. Sitting back down with William they plotted a jump off course which would cut corners rather than be ridden at speed, so it looked as though she was following the all-important team orders.

Second to go she set a fast time and made it look easy. She got a big round of applause and walked Allie off while the other four jumped. Sonja went into the lead, galloping through the finish, and Georgie ended in second place, much to her delight.

"Well done Sonja," she said. "I'm really pleased for you. I knew Evergreen could jump that clear and you did well against the clock."

Helping to get everything packed up, Jane went to pay the bill and discovered that, again, they were leaving the show in credit. The placings that Allie was getting in these high prize money classes were making a huge difference, but she knew that while the stabling and class entries were covered, the overall costs such as diesel, lorry maintenance and groom costs were not. It wouldn't be until she was jumping horses at a much higher level that there would be any chance of that.

Two more team trials followed, one at Wales and West and the other at Vicarage Farm in Surrey. She posted double clears in both, always finishing in the top three without seemingly going against the clock. As the summer wore on, she was gaining in confidence, and decided the final two trials, both being held at the Royal Show in Warwickshire, would be where she really showed the selectors how good the partnership was.

Chapter

13

The Royal Show

Across the country there are a number of county agricultural shows that have been allowed to use the title 'Royal' and the one at Stoneleigh Park in Warwickshire was one of these. Held at the beginning of July each year, the show itself had been running since 1839 with only a couple of 'gaps' during the War years.

It boasted a great all grass arena, where both pony and horse jumping were high on the agenda and with crowd numbers well over 100,000 across the four days, Georgie knew the trials were going to be a big event. The Royal brought together all aspects of farming, food and rural life from the best of British livestock to the latest business and technological innovations in the farming industry and it was quite common to come across a parade of bulls, or herd of pigs, traversing many of the walkways as you made your way to the collecting ring.

The weather was fine and sunny and she could feel

the atmosphere was electric as her class was called. The general public often preferred to watch the pony classes because they were guaranteed a group of riders all keen to beat one another, putting their pony's hooves to the floor to try and win the class.

Georgie was ready to walk the course and knew several of her sponsors were there to watch. Although she had jumped double clear in all three trials she had taken part in, today's and tomorrow's were key, with the team being announced the following day.

William had travelled up to help again and was competing himself in an ABC handicap after her class and the senior grand prix the following day.

All of the competitors were huddling together in their own groups, either with parents or trainers. This time there was no joking between the riders, everyone was taking this very seriously and hoping they were going to do well.

Georgie hadn't eaten all morning, despite everything, she was nervous. She still knew that if things went badly, were she to fall off, for example, she could lose a place in the team.

She'd ridden Allie for 30 minutes at the back of the showground earlier on. It was much quieter there, with the grounds running across to Stoneleigh Abbey and the River Avon running through the farmland at the back. Allie had enjoyed the open spaces and had even thrown in a few bucks, a sign that she was feeling good.

"Competitors walk the course," boomed out over the collecting ring and Georgie and William set off at a pace, wanting time to walk the 14-jump course twice.

The first fence was a triple bar, unusual right at the start, but five paces further, on a slight uphill gradient, was the first vertical, with red postboxes as the wings. Then it was a dog leg to a double of verticals, set at the maximum height, and a gallop to the open water, with no fence in front of it and a dark blue dye leading to it sparkle in the sun. The reflection on the water might startle a few, but Allie had always cleared open water with ease.

Four strides later and there was a set of wavy blue and white planks, then it was round to the left to the combination, a vertical, one stride to an oxer and two strides to a second oxer. They were just over half-way round by now.

Next came a true oxer, where the front and back rails are the same height, making it hard for the pony to judge the width of the fence, again built to the maximum height and width.

A long canter to the top of the ring took them to another set of planks, these were white and set on flat cups, so would be easy to dislodge. Then the last line, an oxer, vertical and vertical.

"The time will be tight Georgie. It will catch a few out," said William. "This is a big ring, a bit like the main arena at Hickstead, and it's easy to be edged into taking wider lines and extra strides. You must ride tight lines and move forwards all the way round."

She knew the time would be tight and also knew the undulating ground would add to the chance of it taking longer to navigate the course. She always rode Allie forward, the mare was so careful in front, so she was fairly certain she could make the time.

William had been absolutely right. The first three competitors all had time faults, so the time was slightly adjusted. But it was still tight.

Sonja and Evergreen were the first partnership with real team hopes to go. Georgie was certain they had a chance; they had notched up one four fault round to date in the trials and wanted to jump double clear today to increase their chances.

The chestnut gelding looked to be jumping well until about three strides from the open water. Whether it was a reflection on the surface, or the fact there wasn't any kind of a ground line in front of the large stretch of open water, Georgie didn't know. But Evergreen threw in what would be called a 'dirty stop' and it took all of Sonja's skill to stay on board. Had she fallen off, that would have meant immediate disqualification.

She gathered her reins, gave Evergreen a smack down her neck and turned to the fence again, pushing her forward with her seat and heels and shouting encouragement. Unfortunately, the same thing happened again, three strides out you could see she was having nothing of it. This time her resistance was earlier, but Sonja was so committed to jump the fence, she fell off, landing on her feet almost in the water.

Leading her pony out of the arena and into the collecting ring, Georgie could see her friend was distraught. She couldn't afford to be distracted now, as there were just two to jump before her, but she vowed she would find Sonja in the stables later.

Suddenly it was her turn. Cantering into the collecting ring she realised how many people were watching this class. The grandstand to the right was full, and the bank along the left-hand length of the arena, where the judges box was set high above the ground, was packed with families enjoying a day out and perhaps hoping their children would be jumping at this level in years to come.

Riding over to the judge's box and saluting, as usual, she heard her name called out and that of her pony. Looking round the course as the clocked ticked down the 45 seconds to when she had to go through the start, she made a mental note of the places she could make up time and the number of strides she was planning on taking between each fence. This wasn't a course where you could add strides: wherever possible you had to take them out.

In no time at all Allie was flying round the course. Throwing in a buck before the double of verticals,

Georgie reprimanded her with a kick and, as Allie lurched forwards, surprised, she worried she'd got too close to the fence. Allie saw where she was, adjusted her approach and cleared both fences with ease.

The water was no problem, as Georgie had suspected, but as she came to the final line she was worried about the time. She heard a whistle from someone in the crowd – not allowed but often heard – and feared it was someone telling her to get a move on. As she jumped the last, she pushed her mount forwards, stopping the clock well inside the time.

"I thought I heard someone whistling," she said to her trainer. "I was worried I wasn't going to make the time." William replied: "You were four seconds inside the time, you had no need to worry!"

The rest of the class resulted in a total of 7 clears from the 36 starters, and four of those were from riders, including Georgie, who were on the team shortlist. The jump off order was read out, the fastest in the first round going last. She was delighted to see she was second to last to go, sixth, as she was determined she was going to pull out all the stops and try and win.

Two of the potential team members were drawn first and third and both jumped steady double clears but left room for their times to be beaten. The second and fourth riders had four faults and eight faults respectively, and the fifth to go, Sally on her cremello gelding, went fast and clear, not turning up tight but really covering the ground. She was the one to beat.

Georgie rode into the grand ring full of confidence, and gave Allie a couple of pats on the neck. "We want to win this one girl," she said. "I want to prove to the selectors we can not only jump clear, but we can win, win against the best here. Then, when we go to the Europeans, we'll have to beat the best there too."

Georgie set off as she meant to go on, galloping through the start and making it clear to her pony this was a speed to maintain. She took all the short cuts her trainer had suggested and one more of her own choosing, meaning she had to cut diagonally across an up-to-height vertical to turn inside and get straight for the next.

It was as though Allie relished a challenge. She sped round the course, kicking her heels high above the poles and, the more Georgie asked, the more she got. Stopping the timing at 29.7 seconds, she knew she was going into the lead by two seconds, a big lead at this level.

She went into the collecting ring and let the groom pop a cooling rug on to her back as she walked her slowly around the smaller sand arena. The Chef d'Equipe came over to congratulate her on a 'great round' and this time avoided telling her off for 'going for it'. She could see Georgie and Allie were now a true partnership and, in a funny way, remembering her own showjumping career, respected her will to win.

The final rider had nothing to lose, so had decided to throw everything at beating Georgie. He looked to be going quite well and was in touch with the time until he came to the double when his mare hit the back bar going in and the front bar going out.

Georgie gave a huge sigh of relief and started to come to terms with the fact she had not only won her first team trial but, as well as heading the Paul Fabrications lead through the winter, had also won their Grand Prix.

It was the first time for such an achievement.

Many ponies were better indoors (for the League) or outdoors for the Grands Prix. This partnership had won both... a win that would go down in showjumping history.

She found herself surrounded by riders offering her their congratulations, recognizing what a moment this was. At the same time she had a journalist from Horse and Hound wanting to interview her and the local radio asking her to go to their on-site studio to record a piece.

She left Allie to go back to the stables with Lizzie and asked her mum to go with her for the interviews. She was a PR professional, with her own company based on the showground, and would make sure she didn't put her foot in her mouth!

Once the interviews were done, she found time to watch William pick up a valuable third place in the evening's ABC handicap before going back to the horsebox in the stable field for supper. She was aiming for an early night as she had another big class the next morning.

It didn't take her long to drop off to sleep that night, despite the noise from other groups parked nearby, and she dreamt of realising her dream the next day – confirmation of her place on the European team – from the announcement that would be made the following day.

Tuesday morning dawned sunny and warm, with a few threatening crowds in the distance. Georgie hoped the weather would stay fine and was down at the stables early to check on her pony. Allie was happily munching on her filled hay net looking as though she hadn't a care in the world.

Opening the stable door she walked up to her pony, the pony that had totally turned her career around. Laying her head against her neck she let her nuzzle her pockets, looking for those expected polo mints.

"Today's the day Allie," she whispered. "I know I don't have to tell you how important this is. Our future together rests on this along with our chances of European success. There's still a long way to go, but we have to jump double clear today. It's more important than all the other times I've talked to you. No bucking, no playing... this is for real."

Leaving her groom to brush her over until her coat

gleamed, pick out her feet, apply the dark black hoof oil, tack her up and walk her up to the collecting ring, she went along the pathway that led to the collecting ring. Feeling the butterflies start to fly around in her stomach she stopped, giving herself a good talking to.

"Today's not a day to be nervous. I need to ride at my best. I have to believe in myself and Allie, this is no time to worry or mess up. As long as I believe I can win."

She arrived ringside while the course was still being built and joined a group of team hopefuls who were getting a last-minute pep walk from the Chef d'Equipe.

"All the work you've put in together over the summer comes to a conclusion today," she said. "Unfortunately, some are going to win and some will lose. You all understand we have to pick the best five combinations to take to Hartpury. The result today is important, but the results across all the trials this summer will be taken into account.

"I know you've all tried your best. I know the hours of training and work that have got you to this point today. All I can add is to wish you luck and hope you all come home safely.

"Whatever your results today, I'll see you in Georgie's mum's office on 10th Street at 4.30pm this afternoon. That's where we will make the team selection announcement. Immediately after this there will be a press conference with the five who will be travelling to

Gloucestershire in late August."

The dates for the championships were already etched in Georgie's mind. She'd had them ringed on the calendar next to her bed since the start of the year. And she'd made herself a daily countdown to the start, which had begun 260 days out. Now she knew she was at day 70. All she had achieved in this year had been aimed at these five days.

"The course is open to walk" boomed out over the tannoy. Walking with William, Georgie could see this was quite a different course from the previous one. The open water was flagged 'out' and instead there was a Liverpool – two vertical poles above a tray filled with water set back from the front poles. In addition, there was a double of water trays, another triple bar, and a combination which was made up of two square oxers as fence one and three, and a tall vertical in the middle.

Georgie knew the combination would cause problems. The distance from the first oxer to the vertical was short and most ponies would have to open up to jump the back bar, then quickly go back on their hocks to jump the vertical clean. Then the distance was long to the oxer out, again this would create a need for very accurate riding.

This time she noticed there were a lot more flags and flowers decorating the arena. Many of them were blowing in the wind that had picked up as the clouds gathered overhead. She was drawn late in the class today and hoped the wind would keep the rain off until the class was over.

Sticking closely to William and listening to his sage advice as they walked the class, Georgie noticed a crowd of people gathering by the curved wall. Trying not to be distracted, she couldn't help but notice an ambulance making its way into the arena.

She carried on walking, but as she went through the finish, walked over to join the crowd by the wall. To her horror she saw one of her friends, 14-year-old Louise, who often travelled to the same shows as her collapsed in a heap on the ground.

The ambulance team were talking to her, gently removing her hat, and calling for a stretcher. She watched while they lifted her on to the metal structure, lifted into the back of the ambulance and started to move slowly out of the ring.

"What's happened?" she asked, to no-one in particular. One of the stewards saw her concern and said: "She just fainted, fell straight to the ground, then had some kind of a fit. We think it's epilepsy. Don't worry, she will be fine. Maybe the pressure was just too much for her today."

Georgie knew Louise's parents had great ambitions for their daughter and had bought her several top ponies earlier in the year, putting her up on to 148s a year early to try to get her on to the Europeans. She also knew, from private conversations she had shared with her, that Louise didn't really want to be a showjumper. She was doing it to keep her parents happy and fulfill their ambitions, not her own.

It was asking a lot for her to jump these trials. They were the toughest courses she would see and she was not very experienced. To give her credit, Louise had never complained, and always ridden well, but the pressure today had obviously pushed her over the edge.

Georgie had no idea she suffered from epilepsy and hoped she would soon recover, watching her parents anxiously following the ambulance out of the arena, any chance she had of competing today disappearing fast.

There was a 15-minute delay to allow everyone to walk the course twice, then Georgie found herself sitting in the competitors' area of the grandstand next to William, who was telling her to pay attention to how the course was riding. It was hard for her to switch her mind away from what had just happened to her friend, but she knew she had to.

The course was throwing up quite a few problems. At the halfway stage there'd only been two clears, both from potential team members. William had been right that the combination was proving the bogey obstacle and, as she walked with him towards the collecting ring, he was telling her how to ride it.

"Allie has plenty of scope, unlike some of these ponies today," he explained. "People are riding too hard at the first element and then landing too close to the vertical. Or they are going in too slow and not making the width of the oxer. You need to ride it as though it's just a normal fence. Don't alter your approach or your stride pattern. She will clear it with ease – that's why she's such a special pony."

Georgie knew he was right and also knew this was her next moment to shine. Legged up on to her pony, she made sure she put in some good flatwork, with half halts and leg changes, before she jumped the practice fences. She always felt good when she felt her pony soar over the fences before she went into the ring.

As she cantered into the arena, she felt a hush fall over the watching crowds. She hardly heard her introduction but knew the announcer had listed some of her achievements in the year and had noted that she had won the previous day's class by a healthy margin.

The sun peeped out from behind the threatening clouds as she set off, and she marvelled at how fantastic she felt to be soaring through the air, never having to worry about whether she would jump clear or not. She knew how lucky she was to ride this magical pony.

As she approached the combination, she remembered what William had said and sat still, letting Allie get the measure of the fence, and not pushing her or holding her back. She met the oxer on a perfect stride, sat back for the oxer, and allowed herself a slight nudge as she sailed over the wide oxer out. She was clear. The rest of the course posed no problems for this combination, and Georgie was over the moon that she had posted the fourth clear.

The few remaining in the class all had faults, so the jump off was small, just four riders to go against the clock. And she was last to go, in the best possible position.

No pony and rider combination had ever won the two Royal Show classes on consecutive days. Georgie knew this was just another record waiting to be set. And she was going to do it – she was going to win the grand prix.

While William was very confident in her ability, he did worry a little that sometimes she asked every bit of her pony, taking chances in her desire to win. There had been two double clears and one rider had a refusal asking for too tight a turn, so before she went in he had some advice.

"The time is fast, but not unbeatable," he said. "You don't have to go flat out and you don't have to take any chances. Remember the bigger prize is being selected for the Europeans later this afternoon. I'm not suggesting you sacrifice the win, but don't make schoolgirl errors."

Georgie understood what he was saying and, although every instinct in her wanted the win, she knew he was talking sense. But once she heard the bell and she went through the start, she was off with just one thing in her mind... the win.

It was as though everything was meant to happen. Allie always relished a challenge and she could tell from the arena, and crowd, that this was a big occasion. She didn't put a foot wrong, rose to answer every question, and threw a huge buck as they galloped through the finish, four seconds faster than their nearest rival. Georgie threw her arms around the neck of her pony and felt tears pricking the back of her eyes.

"You're just amazing Allie. I don't know why, even in the early days, I ever doubted you," she said. "In this moment I couldn't love you anymore. You're everything I could ever want or need."

Her mother rushed over to her as she came out of the ring. "I wish your grandfather was here to have seen that today," she said. "All your hard work has paid off. What a result.

"Luckily, there's someone taking a video of the rounds, so I must make sure I buy them all and send them to him. He'll be so happy. It was just too far for him to travel this time, but we'll give him a call as soon as the team announcement is made."

Going in for the prize giving, and winning another bright blue rug, Georgie was finding it all impossible to take in. Yes, she'd dreamt of this moment, but there'd always been a part of her that doubted she would get here.

She knew a lot of her rivals thought she had a push

button pony that would win, regardless of the rider, but she knew different. She knew it had taken a long time to build the trusting relationship she now had, and knew that, without her on board, the pony would not be as good. It was down to her accuracy and the confidence she gave her, as much as anything.

Putting her hands on the trophy and remembering to thank the sponsor of the class, she cantered around the outside of the arena and again threw her rosette into the waiting crowd. When she went back to the collecting ring, she was surrounded by the other riders and children from the grandstand were calling her name and wanting to congratulate her.

To her surprise, some were asking for autographs, holding up scraps of paper and the show catalogue. For a brief moment she felt like a rock star... but knew just how much of her success was down to her pony.

Chapter

14

The Announcement

After Georgie had made it back to the lorry, sat down and eaten her favourite cheese and marmite sandwich, and had a long cooling drink, she got showered and changed into a clean shirt and pair of her favourite 'lucky' Sarm Hippique breeches before walking over to her mum's office.

Climbing to the top of the stairs, she saw she was the second rider to arrive and walked out onto the balcony which overlooked the bandstand area. The roadways were packed with visitors making their way around the showground, most blissfully unaware of the huge announcement about to be made.

There was champagne on ice in the corner and fresh orange juice for the riders. There were some canapes to enjoy too, her mother had done her proud.

At exactly 4.30pm, when the riders were all sitting down, the chairman of the selectors, Sheila, got to her feet.

"Welcome everyone. This has been an extremely

157

long summer for you all and I know everyone in this room has been hoping for selection. Sadly, we can only take five riders, four will make the team, and we will announce a non-travelling reserve. Should one of the five not be able to travel, for any reason, this sixth rider will take their place. Apart from that, this rider will be staying at home.

"There are a couple of obvious choices, those who have provided excellent results in the trials and have stuck to team orders and posted double clears. Others may not have been quite so lucky, but the five we're naming in a minute have every chance of beating the best of the European teams and bringing home team gold. That is our irrefutable aim.

"I want to say something to those here today who will not hear their names called out. You have all tried your best, you've travelled up and down the country, and you may feel you have done enough. Please don't despair. Those of you who have another year to go in ponies have another chance next year. And remember, we have the autumn round of Home Pony Internationals that we need to select for, and we can announce we'll be taking a Nations Cup team to Verona in Italy in October. So, there's a lot to look forward to, even though you may not be getting your European dream."

Handing over to the Chef d'Equipe, Sheila sat down and looked at the anxious faces in front of her. None of them seemed to be taking their place for granted. They were all looking nervous, crossing and uncrossing their legs and wringing their hands.

"As Sheila has said," Lorraine started, "I'd like to reiterate that this has been a long summer and that we've had to make some hard decisions. Selection is never easy and some people are bound to feel they have been hard done by or overlooked. The main reason for having the trials is so that we do have a measure against which you can all be judged, equally, and while this is not the only selection criteria, it's fair to say that it holds the largest sway.

"But I won't keep you waiting any longer and will now read out the names of the five team members:
Sally Waters and Viscount
Simon Minster and Danny
Georgie Stones and Allie
Gaynor Collins and Serphant
Robbie Wellings and Kiki
"The non-travelling reserve will be Davey Brown with Carlos."

It took a few minutes for Lorraine's words to sink in. Had she really heard her name read out? Did this mean she was going to the Europeans?

She looked around the room and immediately spotted the tears falling down the cheeks of Sonja's face. She and Evergreen had had some good results. Yes, her father had behaved badly in Church Farm but was that why she had been dropped? Georgie thought it was a lot more likely to be the stop at the water jump the previous day. Water was bound to be in the course and the selectors couldn't have a combination that might be eliminated.

She understood how much this had meant to Sonja and knew this was her last year, so her last chance to make it. She was already 16 and, in December, would move up to riding horses. It was hard, but it was part of the sport and, as she had learnt, you had to be able to take the downs with the ups.

Georgie watched as she, and her parents, quietly left the room.

The six chosen jumped up and hugged each other. In some ways the selection was no surprise and Davey, non-travelling reserve, seemed very happy with his selection. "I didn't really expect to get selected at all," he told the group. "To be fair I thought Sonja would get the place. I've still got another year, she hasn't."

All riders went into a press conference where the journalists were handed a press release that detailed each rider and pony, their age, address, and a synopsis of their careers to date. Georgie grabbed one quickly to keep it as a memento and add it to the ever-growing scrapbook of press cuttings and treasures she was keeping safe.

The journalist from Horse and Hound kept addressing her questions to Georgie. "How do you feel today? You have the best pony in the country – do you think you can win Gold at the Europeans? What is the daily routine for the pony? What does she eat?"

Georgie liked the last question because it enabled her to get in a mention of her sponsor, Spillers, who fed all her ponies. Their competition cubes were regarded as the best and guaranteed to be free of any performance-enhancing drugs that, if a pony was tested and they were found, would mean immediate disqualification and quite possibly a long-term disqualification for the rider and, possibly, the pony.

At the end of the press conference it was back to the stables for a team photo, with the ponies all looking their best, still plaited with their tack gleaming. British Showjumping had provided each with a navy wool rug, emblazoned with the British flag and the words European Pony team on both sides. Each rider was given a plastic, zip-up bag to keep the rug safe – they couldn't be used until the team arrived at Hartpury.

"Right," said Lorraine. "Next Friday I need you all back at Stoneleigh, at our offices, for a clothes fitting. You will be kitted out with blazers, shirts, skirts or trousers and shoes for formal wear. Then you will be given three pairs of breeches, three shirts, a show jacket and a riding hat from the team sponsors. Sarm Hippique has offered a new pair of riding boots to each rider, they need to be sorted now, so you have a chance to wear them in before the competition. This gear must be worn all the time you're at the event.

"You already have the rug, you will also get a branded sweat rug, tendon boots, over reach boots and three white numnahs with the British flag. Again, this is what you must make sure you have at Hartpury. Make sure you don't leave anything behind, but we will have a few extras just in case."

Georgie turned to her mother and said: "I didn't realise this would happen. What do I do about my existing sponsors? They've supported me all year. How do I explain I can't wear their gear?"

Jane could see this concerned her daughter. Georgie was quite unusual in having attracted some big names as sponsors and always tried to keep good communications with them and send them any press cuttings and mentions they got.

"Don't worry darling. They're all big companies and they will expect this. They'll all have had a chance to sponsor the team and will expect those sponsors to get the recognition first. We can make up some signs to put on the stables saying who your sponsor is... and the box is all sign-written with their names and details. I'll call them all later in the week and explain the position."

In all the excitement around the team selection, Georgie had quite forgotten to ring her father and her grandfather. Both had been expecting this result, her record was exceptional, but they were both relieved to have it confirmed.

Chapter

15

The Hearing

Leaving the Royal Showground behind on Wednesday morning, Georgie still felt as though she was dreaming. The last afternoon and evening now seemed a lifetime away and she had been overwhelmed by the good wishes she'd received, some from people she hardly knew.

Her one sadness was the reaction she'd witnessed from Sonja and her parents. Instead of taking it gracefully, as she liked to think she'd have done, they'd decided to lodge a formal complaint with British Showjumping.

They'd printed out all the results from Evergreen's record, good and bad, and compared it to the other ponies and riders selected. They were furious that their daughter hadn't won selection and had every intention of making as big a fuss as they could about the result.

Sonja had confided in Georgie that she was beside herself with embarrassment. On the surface she had to keep face with her parents, but she felt the process was fair. As she was planning to further her career in horses, she didn't want to be known as a troublemaker. She feared this decision by her mum and dad would affect her career going forwards.

Her parents' first step was to go to the press and already local papers were beginning to run stories about the selection, which was very negative as far as the sponsors and selected riders were concerned.

A hearing at BS headquarters was scheduled for a months' time and, while everyone was confident of the outcome, there was definitely a sour taste in the air, with everyone avoiding the family at shows and whispering about them behind their backs.

Every pony's record is kept online, with shows sending results into the BS headquarters, and staff in putting them onto the record, stored on a computer database. The record indicated the show, the class that was ridden, and the result achieved. It was possible to see whether the round was jumped clear or how many faults were incurred or what place was won.

In addition, the selectors had kept notes about each of the team trials, not only recording the faults or clear rounds, but also which fences had caused issues and whether there had been any refusals or 'spookiness' shown at individual jumps.

Only Sonja, her parents, and the selectors were at the hearing. The panel who were to rule included the BS chairman, two other directors and a leading showjumper, completely unrelated to any of the selected members. The chairman had the casting vote should there be a split decision.

Videos were shown of various rounds and it was clear to see that Evergreen had consistently shown a reluctance to jump water throughout the summer. On occasions he'd jumped without hesitation, but the panel could see what the selectors were saying – that he was a risk. There was a general feeling that he was being schooled hard by someone other than Sonja, someone who was getting him to jump water in the day or two before each show.

Once you arrive at an international show, and of course the Europeans, it's impossible to further professional school a pony or horse. There would never be a water to jump in the practice ring, and the selectors feared the pony would refuse, as he had at the Royal, and leave the team with just three riders at a crucial time. Yes, he could have been selected as the fifth member, or been the non-travelling reserve, but had they had to call on him, he could have let the side down.

Looking at the team trial results alone, he was 7th on the 'league' having faulted three times and having two stops.

Sonja's parents were really arguing about the selection of Sally and Davey in front of their daughter. It was true that Sally had competed in fewer trials, partly because of the age of Viscount and their determination to keep him sound, but he had always jumped double clear. Earlier in the season there had been occasions when he had 'run away with' his light and younger rider, but a couple of bit changes had sorted that, and she now had him well under control.

Davey, they felt, had been selected because he was the son of a former Olympic rider, not on his results. They argued that he had also not competed in many trials, was based at an equestrian centre with all sorts of jumps and different arenas available, so had an unfair advantage over the other riders.

After nearly two hours of listening to both sides, the panel went away to discuss their decision. To Sonja it was a nerve-wracking time. She found herself going to the toilet several times before they were told to file back into the room, the result was decided.

"We've spent a lot of time deliberating this case and first of all want to make it clear that our decision is unanimous," said Mark Fotheringham, the BS chairman.

"Looking at the video evidence supplied, it's clear to us that Evergreen does not like jumping water. And there's absolutely no doubt that water will be a key part of the European course.

"His results across the summer have not been as consistent as those recorded by the partnerships selected. Yes he's jumped more, and we've taken that into account.

"We understand the pressure these young riders are put under when it comes to major selections but, in this case, we're all agreed that the right decision has been made.

"We will be issuing a press release to this effect later this afternoon and we all hope you will accept our decision gracefully."

So that was that. Decision made and no further opportunity for Sonja's parents to fight.

Georgie hadn't liked the stigma attached to this complaint, it had, in some way, spoilt the elation she should have felt, as Sonja was a close friend. She knew it had nothing to do with her own selection, but she still didn't like seeing the sport portrayed in the press this way.

Later that evening she phoned Sonja.

"What was it like, what did they ask you?"

"It was actually horrible," her friend confided. "I've never been in a court room, but I think it must have been just like that. I felt as though we were on trial.

"They asked lots of questions about whether anyone schooled my pony at home, how hard we had worked on getting her to jump water, why we had jumped all the trials instead of selecting just a few as others had, and why I felt the selection was unfair.

"I had to side with my parents, even though I didn't want to. They would have been furious if I hadn't said what they wanted. They were very upset with the outcome, they really thought they had a case. I didn't, and I promise I tried to stop them from going for this hearing. I just thought we would look like bad losers."

Georgie tried to console her friend, who she could hear was crying.

"The thing is Georgie no-one wants to talk to me anymore. Everyone avoids me and I hate that. You're the only person I can trust and you've been so loyal through all of this. I hope you don't think we were having a go about your selection."

Georgie assured her she didn't think that for a second.

"People have short memories, Sonja. This has hung around for over a month now, it's been a bit like a dark cloud hanging over the selection process. Now a decision is finalised, and has been made public, people will soon come around. And don't worry, I'll be by your side and I'll encourage the rest of the team to support you.

"I get that not being selected was devastating. I remember seeing your face when the team was read out in mum's office. But you're a great rider, you'll be ahead of me on horses for a year and I know you'll have lots of opportunities on Junior and Young Rider teams, you've already got a fantastic team of horses. Don't let this get to you anymore."

After the phone had been put down Georgie wondered what she could do to get her friend back into the tight knit riding circle and came up with what she thought was a great idea.

Early the next day she started phoning her fellow team members and, to her delight, they all agreed. They knew the complaint had been driven by Sonja's parents, not by her.

After she'd ridden she picked up the phone to Sonja again. This was going to be the hardest part.

"Sonja, we all had a team discussion today to see what we could come up with to involve you in the team. We want you involved.

"You have so much experience, you've been competing a lot longer than me, for example, and I think you have some really valuable tips you could share with us.

"We'd like you to come with us to Hartpury next month, as our friend and advisor. We've got lots of adult help, from Lorraine and Gerald, but there's no-one our age who understands the pressure we will be under.

"We want you to help us to cope with the pressure. Come up with fun activities that will take our mind off the event. Keep us active. Be at the ringside to keep us calm. What do you think?"

There was silence for a few minutes and Georgie feared her friend was going to say no. To be at the championships, without taking part, was a big ask.

"I'd love it," she said. "I can't believe you have all

agreed to this after the way I've behaved. This is the next best thing to taking part. Thank you, thank you, thank you."

Georgie was thrilled, now came the difficult bit, letting the selectors know what the team had agreed. There was no doubt they needed to be happy that Sonja was going to be there for the duration.

She was leaving that communication to Robbie, who had a knack of putting things in the right way. The next day she got the reply she wanted, they were happy to welcome Sonja into the fold (as long as her parents weren't involved) and would book an extra bedroom so she could stay on site. Sonja would have to pay for the room, but Georgie knew that would be fine.

Making the phone call to Sonja to tell her everything had been agreed, and about the bedroom, she could hear the happiness in her friend's voice.

"Georgie I'll never be able to thank you enough for this, I know you were behind it. You've been a true friend and I've got something great to look forward to now. I'm already coming up with ideas.

Chapter
16

The Road to Hartpury

As the summer weeks passed, Georgie's main concern was to keep Allie fit and sound. She couldn't bear the thought that her pony could have an accident of some kind and be pulled out of the team.

Every day either she, or groom Lizzie, went over the mare carefully, feeling for any lumps, bumps, cuts or scrapes, and worrying if there was even the slightest bit of heat in her legs. She was still allowed out in the field, but just for a few hours a day, and they made sure any hacking was done in the company of another pony with the route featuring the quietest lanes and roads.

Competitions were kept to a minimum, and classes kept smaller than the height she would expect to jump in Hartpury. The one exception was a trip to the Great Yorkshire Show, where yet again Georgie took chances in the jump off and came home the winner of the Grand Prix. Her tack room was filling up with sashes and red rosettes and a whole shelf had been cleared off the pine dresser in the living room to host the many cups and trophies she was accumulating.

It was also important that Georgie kept fit and she'd been sent a list of exercise routines to follow in the month running up to the championships. There was no need for her to go to a gym, she could do most of the routines at home, and started running down the lane to the church and back every day, a distance of nearly two miles.

Two weeks before they were due to leave, Georgie woke up to hear Lizzie shouting to her from the stable block. Without waiting to get dressed, she ran down to the yard in her pyjamas, she could hear the urgency in her groom's voice.

"There's heat in both her front legs," said Lizzie. "I'm going to hose them for 30 minutes, and if the heat's still there, we need to call the vet. We can't take any chances."

Something like this was just what Georgie had been dreading. At this point they were three weeks away from the championships. What if this was a serious injury? She cast her mind back to the day before and was trying to remember whether Allie had done anything that could have led to an injury. All she could remember was the moment she leapt sideways as a thrush flew out of a thick hedge as she was trotting down the lane. Surely that wasn't enough to cause this?

The 30 minutes of hosing felt more like several hours to Georgie. Once done, Allie was put back into her stable while the duo waited for another 30 minutes to see whether there was any heat again.

"She's still got a bit of heat. Let's give her a day off. But first of all lets trot her up and down and see how she moves," said Lizzie. Trotting up and down twice, on the lane outside, neither of them could detect any sign of lameness.

"I'm going to ring Justin and ask him to come and check her," said Georgie. "At this point I really don't think we can take any chances. I'll ask him to bring the scanner so we can make sure there's no underlying problem."

Justin confirmed he would come out after the evening surgery in Alton, and told Georgie to keep her in the stable, just hand walking her minutes after lunch. Georgie also persuaded her mum to drive her to the local tack shop so she could buy her some toys to hang up in her stable to stop her getting bored and keep her mind alert. Her favourite was a snak-a-ball that you filled with treats and pushed around in the stable to ease them out, at which point Allie would guzzle them up.

The mood was sombre in the yard all day. Georgie was very scared. It was quite possible there would be an injury and Allie would be pulled off the team.

Just after 7pm they heard Justin's car pull into the driveway. He asked Lizzie to help him with the ultrasound unit he would use and had brought a long extension lead so it could be plugged into the nearest electric point.

Carefully applying some gel to both front legs, he ran the probe up and down each leg slowly and carefully. He said nothing and Georgie couldn't bear the silence.

He seemed to be paying particular attention to her near side leg. He went back to it several times and kept enlarging the pictures on the computer screen.

Eventually he stopped, put the probe away and asked them both to follow him into the tack room.

"Don't look so worried Georgie. It's fine. The imaging in this new equipment is very accurate, and although I can see a little heat, showing up here in red, look, there's no damage and no sign of injury. It's good news."

Georgie rushed out to her mum and dad and hugged them both.

"It's OK, she's OK. I'm so happy we've got Justin. He says she's fine."

After accepting a cup of tea before setting off on his next call, Justin handed out some advice.

"I know you're wrapping her up in cotton wool, but that isn't necessarily the best course of action here.

"From tomorrow I would hose her legs down twice a day and ride her as well as walk her in hand. It's quite possible the heat's there because she's standing in the stable too long. I understand you're limiting her time in the field, but you have to make up for that lack of exercise time in other ways.

"She's been an incredibly sound and sensible pony ever since you've had her. Just trust her and yes, take some precautions, but don't leave her in the stable most of the day."

As they watched Justin leave, Georgie and Lizzie decided to write up a new plan of activity that would make sure his advice was followed. It meant more work, but there were two of them, and Georgie knew his advice was sound.

With a little over a week to go before leaving for Hartpury there seemed to be an endless list of jobs to complete.

All of Georgie's clothes were going to be checked to make sure they were perfect. There was her new team jacket and her usual one. She was taking a total of six show shirts, as well as some casual shirts. Her breeches, including her 'lucky' ones were being carefully checked over and any small holes repaired. She had her blazer and skirt needed for the parade and civic reception cleaned and had also packed two pairs of casual trousers and a dress. The final clothes to go in were two outdoor jackets, both needed in case it rained. By now the lorry wardrobe was packed tight.

Her new boots were polished until you could see your face in them, and a pair of wellies, a pair of jodhpur boots and a pair of casual shoes put into the bottom of the cupboard.

All the bedding for Lizzie was added as she would be sleeping in the lorry while Georgie was in one of the student rooms at the college.

Then it was time to go through all the tack needed for Allie, with spares where necessary. Thankfully they had sat down and written a list before they had travelled to Hagen, and had now added a few extra items suggested from their experiences there.

Several rugs went into the rug rack, including a rain sheet, Thermatex rug, sweat rug, stable rug and the show rug she'd been given. Then came bandages, fetlock boots, overreach boots – all with spares. The saddle and bridle went in last, with spare stirrup leathers, spare martingale, an extra snaffle bit and bridle pieces. Two girths were added along with the numnahs that had been packed in a special polythene zip up bag to keep them clean.

Finally, there was Allie's feed and bedding for the week, stacked in a spare partition in the lorry, and her grooming kit. Lizzie added the studs often required if the ground was wet and the blacksmith was coming out a few days before they left to replace all her shoes with ones with stud holes.

The lorry was filled with water and diesel and given a thorough clean, inside and out, so it shone in the sun.

Lizzie had packed her suitcase and popped it in one of the outside lockers, and Jane had made some sausage rolls, scotch eggs, pies, and a lasagne, and packed snacks in the kitchen cupboards and fridge. Most of the meals would be supplied for them all, but it was always good to have some food in reserve.

Suddenly, as an afterthought, Jane thought she'd better pop down to the local Sainsburys and buy some coke and soft drinks and, being optimistic, a couple of bottles of champagne to share with the team, whether they won or lost.

Lizzie was driving the lorry down to Gloucestershire, and Georgie and her mum following a day later, once Allie was settled. They wanted to be on site as soon as they could be, making sure they could find their way around, meet up with the other team members and let Allie have a good look at her surroundings.

That last night before departure Georgie hardly slept, or that's how it felt. She sat and talked to her sister for hours, both of them sharing stories about the ponies they'd ridden and fallen off, with Vikki keen to be as involved as she could. She'd been out in the yard most of the week, helping to clean all the tack, rolling bandages and checking everything was loaded against the list.

They watched one of their favourite horsey films together, Black Beauty, and at the end, after a few tears, agreed it was time for sleep. They had an early start the following morning to travel to Hartpury and Georgie knew she was going to get wound up and nervous once she was on site. Vikki told her sister that she was really proud of her and confident she'd come home with gold medals. She'd already earmarked a space in the house where they would go on display...

The journey to Hartpury was uneventful, with Georgie listening to music on her i-phone. She didn't feel like making conversation and wanted to relax. Despite the music playing through her earphones, she found her mind wondering to how the other riders would feel at this point. Were they nervous, confident, worried, excited? Maybe all of those things.

After Hagen the one thing she had promised herself was never to let her nerves get the better of her again. And, so far, that promise had been kept. Georgie knew she had a pony that could win and knew one of the only ways she wouldn't, would be if she let her down. And that just wasn't going to happen.

As they drove through the gates she could see a huge amount of work had been done on the site since she was last there in the spring. Gravel roads had been tarred, flags from all 18 competing nations were flying everywhere, buffeted by the wind, prominent signs indicated where to go, and temporary stables had been built on the car park.

Ponies were walking everywhere and being hand-grazed on the selected grass fields they were allowed to use. She spotted Sally grazing Viscount and shouted hello to her friend from the car window.

First stop was the stables, to find Lizzie and Allie, and she was thrilled when she saw how the Brits had decorated their five stables with flags and bunting. Allie was fast asleep in the middle of the five stables, looking as though she hadn't a care in the world.

All the ponies were going out for some flatwork at 2pm, and Lorraine had called a team meeting for 12 noon. Georgie told her mother she'd go up to the accommodation blocks and find her room so she could unpack. Taking all of her clothes from the lorry, she was careful to load them flat on the back seat so they didn't get creased.

Hartpury was home to plenty of equine students during term time but, other than those who had volunteered to help during the championships, they'd all gone home. Georgie was struck by how modern the student rooms were and was impressed to find a comfortable single bed, en suite shower room and TV in her room. Getting all her clothes into the wardrobe and chest of drawers was quite a challenge, so she decided to leave her show gear in the lorry which was parked close to the stables.

Having a good wash, she put on her work breeches and one of her older shirts, zipping up her outdoor jacket as the weather looked a bit unsettled. She'd checked the forecast for the week and it looked good, but with English weather you could never be certain.

Jumping back into the car they made their way

down to the stables where the team briefing was being held.

The others were already there and talking to Lorraine and, although she was 5 minutes early, Georgie felt late. She noted she would always make sure she was 10 minutes early for each meeting in future.

"Right team, I'm delighted everyone's arrived on time and safe," she said. "I've checked over each of the ponies while you've been settling in and they all seem good. The vetting is at 5pm tonight, and obviously that is crucial, so I want everyone out on the grass arena at 2pm to give the ponies a good bit of exercise to loosen them up,

"Those of you who were in Hagen, we did that there before the vetting. It hasn't been a long journey for many of you, but they've still been standing still for a while." Sally and Simon had travelled from Essex and Robbie from Yorkshire, whereas Georgie from Hampshire and Gaynor from South Wales had had much shorter journeys.

"When you work them outside I want you to work on exercises to loosen them up. Lots of walk work to begin with, progressing to trot and canter work. Change legs and make sure you work both sides of your pony equally. We will watch carefully and if we see anything worrying, we'll call you over. About 30 minutes of flat work should be perfect.

"Once that's over it's back to the stables. I want each

pony gleaming for the vet check, and plaited. All tack immaculate. You must wear your casual uniforms, so blazer, shirt and skirt.

"I can't tell you how important this is. We don't want to lose a combination before we even start. So, make sure you're ready, your pony is smart, and you do the trot up exactly as you've practiced.

"Tomorrow there's a short warm up class starting at 9am, then the qualifier class for the European individual medal starts at 2pm.

"We'll talk again about this in the morning, but when I say I don't want any heroics I mean it. We are not here to win the warm-up, we're here to use it for what it is for – to let your ponies see some of the fences and see the arena. We expect you all to be able to qualify for the individual, it's the first aim for you all."

After the vetting there was the civic reception and Georgie knew all the teams had been asked to attend in fancy dress, which was unusual. Sonja was arriving that afternoon and had put a lot of thought into what 'her' team were going as, making sure she had all the right clothes and props. Other than Georgie, no-one knew what she was planning.

Georgie decided to help Lizzie get Allie ready for the warm-up and, when a loud church clock chimed twice, she was already on board and walking the mare towards the warm up arena.

She'd spoken many words to her pony that day. She

was certain Allie realised how important the occasion was and walking down to the practice ring, she could feel her grow underneath her and noticed how her ears were pricked and she was taking in everything around her.

Starting with some work in walk on a long and relaxed rein, it wasn't long before she moved up a gear and trotted on both reins, practicing half-halts and rein backs. Moving on to canter she was cantering smaller and then bigger circles on both reins as she heard Lorraine shout her name.

"Georgie, come over here a minute. Allie looks really well, I think another five minutes will do. She needs to be fresh for tomorrow when we have two classes, then we've got the individual on Saturday and the teams on Sunday. That's a lot of work, even for a fit pony."

She noticed that Simon with Danny was being told to stop work too and walked Allie back to the stables, again marvelling at her surroundings and feeling the excitement of being at the Europeans. Of actually being there.

When she got back to the stables, she found Sonja looking for her, dragging a large suitcase on wheels behind her. "Georgie I've got some great costumes in here; I just hope the boys are going to cope with my plan. It's going to be a bit of a challenge to get them on board."

They'd all agreed to meet in Georgie's room to try

on the fancy dress and, despite her friendship with Sonja, she'd no idea what was planned. She knew they had all be asked for various measurements and that her mother had been busy with the sewing machine, but that was it.

Sonja was ready for the big reveal. As she unzipped the suitcase, laughter rippled around the room as the five team members suddenly realised they were going out for the night as the pony team's version of the Spice Girls.

Once they got over their initial shock, the boys got right into it, and one by one filed into the bathroom to get changed. Each time someone came out, they were met with cheers and claps, and Sonja was delighted to see all the costumes fitted.

"I didn't bother with shoes or boots, they would have made things very difficult," she said, "especially as the boys aren't used to walking in heels! I thought you could all go bare foot."

Gaynor was going as Ginger Spice, with her red hair tumbling down her shoulders, and was wearing a very tight-fitting dress with the Union Jack emblazoned across the front and back.

Robbie was going as Scary Spice and had a leopard skin pant suit, teamed with an afro-style wig that was huge, and stood out at 90 degrees from his head.

Simon was Sporty Spice and had the easiest costume, a bright red tracksuit with white piping, and a long wig so his hair could be tied up in a ponytail.

Sally looked amazing when she came out of the bathroom. She had long blonde hair and this had been tied up with long pink ribbon into two bunches. She was wearing a classic pink baby doll dress trimmed with faux fur. With her slim build, this worked well, and she got several wolf whistles as she entered the room.

Last up with Georgie who was dressed as Posh Spice. She had a long black wig, and wore the hair lose. This was teamed with a thigh-skimming little black dress that Posh had made famous and was always known for wearing on stage.

The group looked at one another and fist pumped. They couldn't believe what a great job Sonja had done and knew they would steal the show at the reception later that night. Yes, a couple of the dresses were a little risqué, but they were confident they'd get a lot of attention and be supported by their management team who had absolutely no idea what had been planned.

"Sonja you've done an amazing job," said Georgie. "I don't know what to say. We're all so pleased and can't wait to see what else you have planned for us." Her views were echoed by the rest of the group, who realised the decision to get her involved was absolutely the right one. They all packed up their clothes and went back to their rooms, agreeing to meet at the stables at 3.30pm to get ready for the vetting.

Georgie decided to have a quick shower and then get changed. To her horror the water was really cold, perhaps there were too many people trying to shower at the same time.

She knocked on Gaynor's room and found she was experiencing the same problem.

"I'm going to pack up my stuff and go back to the lorry to shower," she said. "Anyone else is welcome to join me." Each rider had come in their own lorry as the show was in the UK, so all agreed this was the best tactic.

Arriving at the lorry she told Lizzie what she was doing and, spotting Lorraine at the end of the row of UK boxes, went over to tell her the problem. "Right, I'll go and find the maintenance team and get them to check this out Georgie. Is it OK if they go into your room and take a look?" Georgie agreed immediately, she didn't want to be facing a cold shower every day!

Coming out of the shower wrapped in a towel, she heard a knock on the door. "Yes," she shouted. Lorraine told her the maintenance team were on their way and had had other complaints and were fairly certain it was a boiler issue that could quickly be sorted.

She got herself dry and carefully put on her 'uniform'. The skirt was quite loose, clearly she had lost some weight – probably due to her nerves – in the six weeks that had passed since it arrived.

Walking across to the stables she could see they had

become a hive of activity. All the riders from different nations were making their way to their ponies, ensuring they looked smart and ready for inspection.

She saw Lizzie, and the second groom Penny, had been hard at work and had woven red blue and white ribbon through each pony's mane and tail. When the show rugs went on, they all looked stunning. Coats gleaming, tack shining, and hooves polished, they made their way down to the veterinary inspection, all praying their ponies would get through.

The first trotted up and down was the grey Kiki with Robbie. "Pass" rang out after the passport had been checked. Next was Sally with Viscount. Another "Pass". So far so good.

Third was Simon with Danny. "Trot up and down again please" said the chief vet, chairman of the panel. Simon did as he was asked, going a little slower this time. "Held" rang out across the silence of the run-up. Looking distraught, Simon walked his pony back towards Lorraine and Gerald.

"How did he look?" asked Simon. "Honestly a little stiff," answered Lorraine. "But 'held' just means held. They'll have another look at him tomorrow. We'll make sure he's done some work to loosen him up before a second vet check. Try not to worry."

But Simon was worried. Although he'd ridden on other pony teams, he'd never been to the Europeans, and this was his last chance., as later in the year he was moving onto horses. He had his career all mapped out in his head and knew a good result would stand him well in the future. Danny was older than the other ponies and tended to stiffen up when left in his stable for a long time. But he'd only been left for a couple of hours after the workout in the morning. What could have gone wrong?

It was Gaynor and Serphant's turn now and they passed, giving the others a huge sigh of relief. Just Allie to go.

Georgie could feel her heart in her mouth as she passed the reins over Allie's head and started to run to the table. Turning around she ran back to her teammates. Walking back they stopped in front of the judges while the passport was checked. To her surprise one of them stood up and reached under the table for a measuring stick.

"Please bring your pony over here," he said to a now very rattled Georgie. "Stand her four square." Georgie did as she was told and was so relieved to hear the vet call out "Dead on 148cms, pass."

Allie was the only pony measured that afternoon. All the team felt she had been picked on as the hot favourite for the individual, but couldn't make a complaint and, anyway, fortunately she was measured 'in'.

As they walked back to the stables together, Lorraine asked them to hand their ponies to the two grooms and to come for a team chat. Lizzie had already been briefed to hose Danny's legs down every few hours and walk him out twice during the night to stop him stiffening up.

"We've had a bit of bad luck today, but I don't want that to worry any of you. I'm sure Danny will be fine in the morning, with Lizzie following my instructions, and it was, I feel, more than bad luck that Allie was measured, but very good that she measured in. Under saddle this mare always looks a bit bigger, but once the saddle is off and she's relaxed, she has always measured in.

"You have a fun night ahead of you, I'm looking forward to see what you are all going to the reception wearing and I want you to enjoy yourselves. But this time, when I say no drinking I mean it." She was looking closely at Robbie and Simon as she said this and Georgie was hoping that, for once, they could behave and follow team orders.

"I'll see you in the marquee at 7pm. There will be plenty of food but, if anyone's hungry afterwards, we can always go to the canteen which is open until 9.30pm, or call for a takeaway. Just let me know."

Georgie was sure she wouldn't be able to eat much and knew she had lots of munchies in her lorry, so wasn't concerned.

Going back to their rooms they had an hour to kill before going down to the reception. Time enough to get into their Spice Girl outfits and put on makeup with Gaynor, Sonja and Georgie agreeing to work on Robbie and Simon as they had no experience in putting on the necessary foundation, eye shadow, mascara and lip gloss.

The atmosphere in the room was one of a mixture of fear, nervousness, excitement and joy. All of the team were experiencing different emotions. But as the outfits went on, and the makeup was applied, their laughter could be heard along the whole corridor.

At exactly 10 minutes to 7 they were ready. They'd already agreed they would walk down in their trainers and wear coats over their clothes, just revealing the Spice Girls image once they were inside the marquee.

Entering together silence fell across the room as the music suddenly changed and the sounds of one of the group's greatest hits, Wannabe, boomed out from the loud speaker. What a music choice – they were all Wannabes, Wannabe European champions. Sonja had even managed to persuade the DJ for the evening to make sure their entrance was noticed.

Throwing aside their coats, the five of them stood in a line as cameras flashed and the other competitors cheered their arrival. The local mayor walked across and congratulated them on their entrance, followed by Lorraine and Gerald, who couldn't believe how they'd successfully taken over the night.

"Let's hope this success tonight continues over the

weekend," she said. "Well done team, and well-done Sonja. I can see how much effort has gone into this and I couldn't be prouder."

A week later this picture, featuring the line-up that included two boys in drag, was featured on the front cover of Horse and Hound, and the team were amazed by the number of letters they received asking for copies of the picture and complimenting them on their bravery that night.

Chapter
17
The Championships

The first job the following morning was to get Danny through his second vet check.

They'd agreed to be with Simon and were waiting patiently by Danny's stable at 8am. Walking round to the trot-up area, they found there were three other ponies that had been 'held', two from France and one from Denmark.

Danny was first to be checked. Everyone held their breath and crossed their figures as he trotted up and down. "Pass" rang out from the chairman of the panel and Georgie couldn't stop herself from shouting a 'hurrah'.

The expression on Simon's face said it all. Relief and joy in equal measures.

Going back to the stables they started preparing for the opening class, a warm up before the qualifier in the afternoon. Lorraine had already decided to withdraw Danny to keep his jumping to the minimum, so Simon was only too glad to help the others get ready.

By the course walk time of 9am, they were all at the ringside to examine the course with Lorraine and Gerald. Georgie could immediately see the course builder had been generous and built at between 1.25m and 1.30m rather than the permitted 1.35m. There were a couple of tricky distances, where you had to be riding forward or holding but, other than those, the team was enthusiastic about the start of the competition.

Georgie had been drawn the first Brit to go, so was seen as the pathfinder, so it was important for her to get the distances right and come back to tell the others how the course went. Going 5th she had time to warm up on the flat and then watch one go before she jumped. The first pony had one down, a careless mistake, rather than a misjudgment.

Hearing her teammates shouting 'good luck' as she rode confidently into the ring, yet again she was aware of the silence that hung over the ground as she saluted to the judges.

The crowds would be bigger that afternoon, but she knew all her main competitors were watching her every move.

This time she followed the team orders to the letter and posted a lovely clear inside the time. Going back to her group she explained the distance from the double of water trays to the planks was a long five, and to push for the five but, other than that said the track rode well.

Lizzie took Allie back to the stables for a rub down and rest before the afternoon's qualifier, while Georgie watched her teammates take their turn. At the end of what seemed a long course, all five had jumped clear, a great and encouraging start.

There were three hours between the two classes, time to kill and settle the nerves and Sonja had come up with a great game for them all to take their minds away from worry over the qualifier.

"I've organised a treasure hunt," she said. "There are 30 items to find within the College grounds. There are some bags and boxes here so you can keep the items safe as you find them. I'm giving you 90 minutes to complete the task and the winner will get a brand- new Whitaker bridle. We need to allow a good hour before the course walk at 2.30, so make sure you're back here in the stable area by 1.30pm at the latest and I'll check off your items. It'd be a good idea if you take a pen and mark off the items you've found."

Casting her eye down the list Georgie found a few things that made her smile. Sonja had been very inventive and challenging. They needed to find an edible berry, a safety pin, a tennis ball, a bra, a horseshoe, some bright red lipstick and a light bulb, amongst a host of other things. Some were harder than the others, and she smiled wondering how the boys were going to collect a bra... it certainly wouldn't be one of hers.

Her strategy was to find the hardest things first and she knew a good place to start was in her room and then in the stable office. Walking around the grounds to find the outdoor items was going to take time.

Keeping her eye on the clock she got back to the stable area with 5 minutes to spare, to find all the others had been checked in and already left to get changed.

She was missing six items – a hedgehog spine, a penknife, a photo of a weeping willow tree, the tennis ball, a calculator and a pair of men's braces. The winner was going to be announced after the qualifier, to give Sonja time to check the results and organise the prize giving.

Back in her room getting changed, Georgie remembered she had had a calculator with her in the lorry as she had some schoolwork to complete. And with more time to think, realised she could probably got a tennis ball from the sports centre on site.

Changing into her new riding outfit for the first time and checking her hair and look in the mirror, she was proud of how smart she looked. Her nerves over the past month had led her to lose some weight and she felt proud to be wearing the Union Jack on her jacket again.

The draw had been posted at lunchtime and again Georgie found herself first to go, in 8th place. This gave her time to watch a couple of others go and she thought perhaps it was good for her nerves not to be later on in the class.

Walking the course she found herself thinking of everything that could go wrong, rather than everything that could go right. This was putting negative thoughts in her head and she stopped, dead, in front of the water and told herself that she wasn't going to make the same mistakes as she had in Hagen. This time she was not going to let her nerves make her lose an opportunity.

The course was big, but no bigger than what she had jumped in the trials during the summer. Maybe the cups were flatter, the poles lighter, and the times tighter, but Georgie was growing in confidence as she walked, believing Allie could jump this with ease.

She could see that the combination had been built with plain coloured poles that would merge into a pony's line of sight and made a decision that she would take a slightly longer line to this trying to give Allie more time to size up the fence.

In no time at all the bell rang and Georgie sat at the ringside to watch the first three go. All had a single, different fence and, as was often the case, it didn't seem that any particular line was causing a problem.

While she was warming up she heard a huge round of applause from the stands and realised one of the French riders had jumped the first clear round. This was followed by a clear from the first German rider – both top countries already showing their colours.

Now it was her turn. She cantered confidently into the arena, heard the bell ring, and started her approach through the timing towards the first fence.

Giving Allie a small nudge with her heels as she approached the first vertical, she was horrified when she heard the resounding 'thud' of a pole as she landed the other side. She didn't dare risk turning around, but she knew the first fence had fallen.

She was completely thrown. So many thoughts ran through her head, all at the same time. Allie was so careful, what on earth had gone wrong?

Her brain went into overload and she started to ride with extreme care. This meant she was slowing down, not riding forward, and trying to meet every fence accurately.

In the team talk earlier, Lorraine had told them all that she felt 4 faults and possibly 8 faults would get them through to the individual, and this single thought was making her determined not to have a second fence down.

As she came towards the final double on the course, two blue and white parallels, Georgie knew that if she jumped those clear she'd qualified. Holding, holding, holding for that perfect stride she suddenly realised she was a few metres from the fence and at the pace she was going even Allie wouldn't be able to jump such a big double. She turned away, incurring a 4-fault penalty for a refusal.

Instead of quickly turning and coming back to the double again, she went a longer route around the water jump to get a good line, jumped it clear and galloped through the finish.

Time is always much tighter in international classes and she knew this. And, as she started to go out of the ring, she heard her score read out over the loud speaker – 8 and a half faults. The half was a time penalty, and she was certain this would mean she failed to qualify.

Lorraine was the first to speak to her in the collecting ring. "That first fence was just unlucky Georgie, she touched it very lightly behind. It bounced out of the cup and then fell. It was the sort of pole that nine times out of 10 would have stayed in place.

"After that you started to ride backwards. I could see you were trying to be ultra-careful. Now we'll have to wait until the end to see whether you've got through. As you know the top 30 qualify. That time fault certainly won't help."

Her teammates were sympathetic and Sonja was soon there to give her a hug and some tissues. "You may be fine, a few are having very bad rounds out there, I think the nerves are really getting to them."

The class seemed to wear on forever. Georgie found herself wishing people to have faults so she could qualify but, at the same time knew that wasn't sportsmanship. Three of the GB riders posted clears, inside the time, with just Gaynor and Serphant being disqualified after two stops at the water... something that had never troubled her pony during the long summer of trials.

As the last rider jumped clear, Lorraine came to her with the bad news. "Unfortunately, you've ended 32nd, so you haven't qualified. Even if someone pulls out you won't get through as the qualification doesn't drop down. Robbie, Simon and Sally are through, and we'll give them all the support we can tomorrow.

"In half an hour I want you all at the stables so I can confirm the team."

Several of the foreign riders came over to share their commiserations. They were all shocked as Georgie had been such a hot favourite for the individual title. But no-one was more disappointed than Georgie herself, who had spent all year building up to this moment, and really couldn't understand how it could have gone so wrong.

Walking across to her mother she couldn't hold back the tears any longer. "I just want to go back out there and jump again. Please go and ask the judges if I can. I've let Allie down again, none of it was her fault. I need to show everyone we can jump round that class clear."

Putting her arms round her daughter Jane realised what an effect this was having on her daughter. Not for the first time, she realised the pressure they had all been living with.

"I'm sorry darling, this is the European

Championships. You only get one chance. There's no way you'd be able to go in that ring again."

Pulling herself together she realised she still had a chance to win gold in the teams on Sunday... if she was selected. She'd soon know whether she was going home empty handed.

Chapter

18

The British Team

All the riders made their way to the stables as Sonja wanted to announce the results of the treasure hunt.

"In fifth place we have Robbie who managed to get 20 items from the list. I'm not sure where he got the bra from," she said, holding up a bright red lacey number. Robbie smiled and started to say "you know that really pretty Swedish girl, Anika, well...." as his story was cheered.

"In fourth place we have Simon with 26 items – no bra – and in third place we have Sally with 27. In second we have Gaynor with 29 and the winner is Georgie with 30. Well done everyone, you all did a great job. I hope you found it fun and it took your minds off the qualifier for a while."

Handing Georgie a tin of Roses chocolates, the teammates gave her a pat on the back and round of applause, which soon petered out as Lorraine started to walk down the stables.

"What's going on?" she asked, quite surprised her

team were in such good spirits.

"I've just awarded the prize to the treasure hunt winner, Georgie," said Sonja. "She's got a big tin of Roses that I'm sure she'll share with us all. It's time for a chocolate fix!"

As Georgie opened the tin and passed it around, Lorraine and Gerald suggested they all sat down on the hay bales outside the stables.

"First of all, well done to the three of you who've qualified for the individual tomorrow. We haven't got the start order yet, but we'll have it by 6pm. Keep your eye on the notice board at the end of this building and then we'll have another meeting at 7pm before we go to dinner.

"The team for Sunday is the following and will ride in this order.

"First Robbie with Kiki, second to go will be Sally with Viscount, third Georgie with Allie and last will be Simon with Danny. Robbie makes a great pathfinder, and Simon, if we're lucky enough to all jump clear, your pony might not have to jump twice. As he's in the individual tomorrow we need to keep him fresh."

Gaynor was the one left off the team and no-one was surprised after her elimination at the water in the qualifier. Serphant had been checked over by the vet after that class and was slightly lame on her off fore. The selectors had felt there had to be something wrong as water jumps had never been a problem in the past.

"Tomorrow we will all be ringside to cheer Robbie. Simon and Sally on in the individual. Georgie, only light work for Allie tomorrow morning, with just a few jumps to keep her sweet. There's a nice track through the forest at the back of the stables and it might be good to let her have a walk around there first thing to give her a change of scenery."

Georgie went to talk to Gaynor, who was very philosophical. "I knew I'd be dropped," she said. "They can't take a chance and I don't want to make a minor injury worse by jumping him anyway. It's horses I'm afraid... just the luck of the draw. All I want is for us to take home gold medals on Sunday and show these German and Dutch teams that Great Britain's the best!"

Later that evening Georgie got showered and changed into the dress she'd bought for the formal dinner, which was being held in a local hotel. It seemed so strange to her to be wearing a dress and heels when 95% of the time she was wearing breeches or jogging bottoms. She hardly every wore make up, but she knew tonight she had to look her best.

Some of her sponsors had bought tickets to the dinner and would be sitting on the table with her, so she needed to prove she could communicate well and keep the conversation going, and she was up to the task of dressing up when needed.

Walking into the dinner together, the team members went to their respective tables and soon settled into conversations. Georgie's sponsors were disappointed she hadn't made it through to the class the next day, but understood how tough this level of competition was, and were delighted to be there to support her on the team on Sunday.

Calling it an early night, she was back in her room soon after 10pm but was kept awake for another hour by riders running up and down the corridor, banging on doors, loud music playing and a lot of shouting. Eventually she popped in the earplugs she'd anticipated she might need and drifted off to sleep, dreaming about wearing a gold medal round her neck.

The next morning, after she'd ridden Allie round the forest track and done some schooling in the arena, she got dressed into her uniform and walked down to sit with her mother in the stands. All the parents were together and tension was mounting as the start to the class got closer.

Georgie and Gaynor were allowed to walk the course and saw this as a great experience. It was certainly up to height from the very first fence, 1.35, and Georgie knew it could go up again for the jump off. Listening to the advice Gerald and Lorraine were giving, she found herself wishing that she'd made it this far.

It wasn't long before the bell rang for the first competitor and, as the class went on, Georgie found herself getting more and more frustrated as the poles fell all around the arena. In the end only four riders had jumped clear, the only British rider was Simon with Danny.

The course was shortened and four of the fences went up again, this time reaching the maximum height allowed. Danny was drawn last, so had the best draw, but as he was the smallest of the ponies the fences looked huge.

The first to go, the Swedish rider Anike Fookstrom, who'd gained the attention of Robbie as soon as he set eyes on her, jumped quickly but had the last fence down. The second, a French rider Simon Balestre, jumped clear. The third rider, a German, Hendrik Sommerman also jumped clear but was a little slower than Simon.

You could hear a pin drop as Simon rode confidently into the arena. He saluted to the judges and, once the bell had rung, was on his way. Halfway round the course he was still clear and the Brits in the grandstand had linked hands and were willing Danny to jump clear.

As he turned to the last line something spooked him and he jumped sideways, losing his rhythm. Simon got him back on track but rolled the top bar from the first part of the double, and there was a huge thud as it hit the ground.

The crowd gasped. Would he get the bronze medal with third place, or was his time slower than Anika's? Danny was nearly a hand, or four inches, smaller than her pony and Georgie was worried his time would be slower.

"That's third place and the bronze medal to British rider Simon Minster with Danny," said the announcer. "Fourth place goes to Anike Fookstrom with Candyman."

The Brits stood up and cheered as Simon left the arena. When the three medalists had got their rugs and sashes and came back into the ring for the presentation, the National Anthems were played, with the loudest singing coming from the British supporters.

Once he had the medal around his neck and had galloped around the arena waving at the crowds, Simon's face was a picture of happiness. His usual ice cool demeanor was gone and back was the 15-year-old boy who was just so happy to have achieved one of his ambitions.

His teammates were quick to congratulate him, and reward Danny with polos and carrots they all had in case of the win.

Danny was lost for words and was even interviewed by the BBC who had sent a regional film crew as the championships were on home ground.

Once the celebrations were over, it was back to the stables to take the horses out for a hand graze of the luscious grass surrounding the arena and then time to get changed again for the disco and karaoke evening in the big marquee behind the far side of the arena.

Yet again Sonja had something planned and had been coaching her group to sing three songs:

Congratulations (this would have been pulled if one of the rider's hadn't won)

White Horse (Taylor Swifts big hit) and

A Horse with no Name (made famous by America)

They all knew they were going to sound awful and completely out of tune, only Gaynor had anything resembling a voice that anyone would want to listen to!

But when the time came their practice had made it as perfect as it could be and they got a huge round of applause and cheers as everyone in the marquee joined in on the choruses.

At 11pm the disco came to a halt, everyone realising that an early night was needed before the team event that would start at 2pm the following day. Lorraine walked them back to their rooms and made sure they stayed put before leaving for her hotel. She was quietly confident about her team and wanted to ensure they had an early night before the challenges of the next day.

Chapter

19

Teams

Sunday morning dawned bright and sunny, with a gentle breeze flapping the nations' flags dotted around the arena. Lorraine had told her team to be down at the stables by 9am to give the ponies a good stretch before 10am so there was plenty of time for the grooms to bath, dry, plait and prepare so they each looked immaculate for the parade.

Georgie was the first one down to the yard. She'd managed to eat a piece of toast and gulp down a cup of tea, but anything else was just too much for her to manage. She knew her nerves were beginning to get to her and gave herself a good talking to. She needed to trust Allie more than ever today and be certain she gave her best performance for the team.

Walking into her stable she saw the mare flick her ears forward and heard her give a gentle nicker. Reaching in her pocket for the familiar polos, she talked to Allie as though she was her best friend.

"I know I've said this to you before, but today really

is our most important day. Now we have to show Europe, not just Britain, what we're made of. This is going to be the hottest competition we have been in and every jump and every second will count. I'm going to put my total trust in you and we're going for gold."

She watched the other team members following the same sort of routine. At this level the partnership between horse and rider was key and each of them had their own way of communicating to their mounts.

Waiting for Lizzie to finish tacking her up and checking over the tack for what felt like the hundredth time that week, she quietly led Allie out into the sunshine and was legged up into the saddle.

Once she was riding she felt the tension and nerves melt away and immediately felt at one with her ride, letting her dictate the pace. She certainly felt fresh, throwing in some bucks as she cantered round, so Georgie worked her for an extra 10 minutes, knowing she needed the mare's complete concentration that afternoon.

Back in the stables there were two hours to kill before they needed to be dressed and ready to walk the course before the parade. Cars had started to arrive and, with the lovely weather, picnics were being laid out on the grass and there was a really festive atmosphere.

Sonja had recognised this would be a tough time for the new team members, waiting for something to start was always hard. It was when you allowed your thoughts to run over all sorts of things that could go wrong, rather than to focus on the positive things that could go right.

She called the team and Gaynor together and handed them all some printed sheets. "I've worked on an equestrian quiz for you all," she said. "There are some simple, and some harder questions, and we're all going into Robbie's lorry to sit quietly and answer them. No cheating allowed – I'll be there to make sure you don't use your phones to look up the answers."

What she didn't say is that she had worked with Georgie's mum Jane, and Robbie's mum Fiona to organise some tasty snacks and drinks that would be in the lorry too. Lorraine had told her she didn't want anyone jumping on an empty stomach, running the risk of feeling feint, coupled with nerves, could become a disaster.

They had been busy visiting the local supermarket earlier and coupled the snacks they had sourced there with some that had been brought the previous evening by the other mums. There were snack size sausage rolls and scotch eggs, a salmon quiche, some cheese and egg tarts, bowls of popcorn and crisps and some delicious looking strawberry and raspberry mini sponge cakes.

As Lorraine had predicted, the riders tucked into the snacks almost without realising while filling in the quiz answers. With 50 questions, some requiring a lot of brain power to answer, the hour flew past and, before they knew it, it was time to go back to their rooms to get changed. They left the papers with Sonja to mark while they got ready.

At exactly 12.30pm, as instructed, the four team members were dressed and ready to walk the course. Georgie had got to the arena 15 minutes before the others and had watched the final touches put to the course. There were more flowers than she'd ever seen and a big open water with just a little brush in front of it, a fence that would stop quite a few. It was in a place where the sun reflected brightly on the blue water and she could see from the ringside this would be a bogey.

Gaynor was walking with them and immediately spotted this challenge. "I'm so glad we were dropped," she said. "I couldn't have borne it if we had stopped or I had fallen off."

As the bell rang to announce the opening of the course, the team set off with both Lorraine and Gerald carefully walking out the distances between each fence.

It was up to height, had very flat cups and light poles in places, making it easy for a pole to fall, and had some difficult distances – places where riders were going to have to decide whether to take an extra stride or, knowing their pony, push for the three or four.

There was a double of verticals at maximum height. So flimsy and gappy that Georgie thought the wind, which was picking up, could blow them down. The water was just a short five strides to a set of white planks, both of which would need some jumping.

The course used the whole arena and Lorraine was quick to tell them that time would be tight. They needed to plot their lines carefully and not allow themselves to drift adding in strides as they went.

Walking together first as a team, they then went round again in their own time. Georgie felt her confidence growing. There wasn't anything she hadn't jumped before and she felt Allie was more than up to the job. The question was, was she?

Back in the collecting ring they all mounted up and riding four abreast followed Lorraine into the arena. She was carrying a union jack flag, on a long pole, leading her team first around the arena. Followed by the other nine competing nations, the parade made quite a sight and, as the Brits rode past the grandstand, a huge roar and cheer echoed around the site.

The draw had put Great Britain in fourth place. First to go were teams Sweden, The Netherlands and Switzerland. Following Britain were France, Germany, Belgium, Spain, Italy and Ireland. A team from Portugal had entered but, with two ponies failing the vet check after the individual, were unable to field a team.

The British team were huddled together in a corner, the ponies all wearing their bright blue rugs. "Now everyone, this is what we've come here to win," said

Lorraine. "We have to keep it together and our aim is to jump four clear rounds twice. Don't think this will be easy, especially in the second round, but all your ponies are good enough and there's nothing out there they haven't seen before. We need positive, forward, riding, and we need you to let your pony jump."

Georgie was surprised she didn't feel more nervous, but for once she was confident and looking forward to her chance to shine.

But she was soon to feel the nerves kick in as the first three riders all had fences down.

First to go was Robbie with Kiki, the pathfinder. He had watched the first to go and knew there hadn't been a clear round. That was added pressure, but he was more than up to the task and had his father there passing on some valuable tips and lines to take - the sort of support that can only come from someone who's jumped all over the world for many years.

A hush fell over the arena as he cantered into the arena. Someone shouted 'Come on Robbie' as he went to salute the judges, but the call never resonated. He was already completely concentrating on the job in hand.

Sally, Georgie and Simon stood together, arms linked, each with fingers crossed. In under two minutes it was over, Robbie had jumped the first clear round.

The British crowd in the stands jumped to their feet

and furiously waved the Union Jacks they'd brought. As Robbie came out of the arena, he was congratulated by all, and jumped off Kiki who was going back up to the stables for a break while the rest of the competition carried on.

At the end of the first round, with all nine nations fielding a team member, there were just two clears, Robbie's and one from the first German rider. This was the start they had hoped for.

At the start of the second round the Swedish rider jumped clear, while the Dutch rider had a stop at the water, but jumped it the second time, and the Swiss rider had 8 faults and a time fault.

Time for Sally and Viscount. Again, there was a huge cheer from the crowd as she entered the ring, and Viscount reacted by jumping sideways and nearly unseating his rider. Gathering up the reins and giving him a quick slap down the neck, she went through the timing and was off. The crowd reacted with joy again – a second clear for the home nation.

At this early stage of the competition the biggest threat seemed to be coming from Germany and that continued as the second rider jumped clear. At the end of the second round the first two teams tying were Britain and Germany, with Spain in third place with four faults in the first round, and a clear in the second.

Now Georgie was up on Allie, and working her way through her usual warm up. As the fences in the practice ring went up, she could feel her mare concentrate and her confidence grew as she felt her soar through the air. She felt as though she had springs on her feet and, touching a 1.35 vertical in front, she gave it a good 10cms when she came back to it a second time.

"That's right girl, we don't want to touch the paint," she said, giving her a good pat.

As the rope was lowered for her to enter the ring, she heard the good wishes from her teammates, and then blocked out all noise as she prepared to jump for gold.

There wasn't a second's hesitation from her mare. As she followed the lines she had worked out in her head, the mare jumped better and better. At the water, she soared over the blue pool to 'ohhs' from the crowd, and easily picked up at the white planks which had been causing quite a few problems.

Coming to the double of verticals she kept riding forwards this time. She trusted this feisty mare and knew she could jump them clear. As she galloped through the finish a few seconds later, she heard the words she wanted to hear 'clear round, inside the time. That's clear round number three for Britain'.

Now Lorraine had to make a decision. And it wasn't easy. In theory there was no need for Simon and Danny to jump, they couldn't improve on their zero score. But could she risk not letting him see the fences and jump round as he might be needed in the second round?

After chatting with Gerald and Simon, she decided not to jump him. It was a tough decision and only time would tell whether it was the right one.

As there was an hour-long break between the two full rounds, the ponies were back in the stables out of the sun and having a rest before being asked to jump again. Lorraine was busy impressing on the team how the second round was always harder and how four of the fences were going up, including the planks after the water and the last double of verticals.

She made sure they all had some drinks and ate a couple of sweet biscuits before taking them all back to the ring to look at the altered fences.

As the ponies started to come down to the collecting ring, Sally, Robbie, Georgie and Simon were standing together talking about the next round. "We've got a real chance here," said Robbie. "I know we're equal with the Germans at the moment, but I know we can smash this. We just need to keep our nerve. The ponies are all on great form, it's only if we, as riders, make mistakes that we won't win."

That wasn't exactly what Georgie wanted to hear and she felt those always present butterflies making their return trip to her stomach. Seeing her looking worried, Sally put her arm over her shoulder and said: "Robbie's always full of confidence and often says things without thinking Georgie. You've done great. We can only do our best. Any one of us can lose concentration for a second and knock a fence. Trust Allie, she's the best."

It wasn't long before a long ring of the arena bell signalled the start of the second round.

Again, four faults was posted by the first and second rider, this time at different fences, and the Swiss rider had 12 plus time faults. That looked as though it would be their discard score.

Robbie was next and knew a clear round would keep the team in pole position. Kiki jumped out of her socks, easily clearing the heightened fences, and leaving the ring sporting a huge grin, he heard the crowd cheer as the first double clear was recorded.

The second German rider also posted a clear, so the teams were neck and neck and the tension was mounting. Cantering into the ring, Sally knew all the pressure was on her and Serphant now and heard the crowd gasp as a toe in the water led the two water judges to jump to their feet and wave their flags. As she started to leave the ring she heard the words 'Four faults, Great Britain' and felt her eyes well. She'd been the one to let her team down.

The others rushed to her side and told her she had done a great job. Supporting each other as always, they all understood how it must feel to be the first one to have a fence down.

After the second German rider had also posted a clear, the pressure was growing even more. Georgie refused to let this get to her and consciously blocked everything out, even the shouts of support from the crowd and her team.

Leaning down to Allie's ears, really believing she could understand, Georgie told her what had happened and that her upcoming round was vital. They just had to jump clear.

She had never felt this much pressure in her life, and she really didn't want that to get through to her mare. Summoning an inner strength she didn't know she had, when the time came she trotted confidently into the ring and focused on the job in hand.

Halfway round she felt something wasn't quite right. Was it her imagination or did Allie feel unlevel between the fences? She looked down after the planks and saw to her horror that one of the overreach boots was flapping around her fetlock. Somehow she must have caught it with her hind hoof and it was torn.

Not knowing what to do, she realised she had no option but to continue. They couldn't risk a bad round or elimination. Talking to Allie as she continued, she became absolutely determined she would get through the finish. She wasn't going to face another tack failure, even though this one was completely different from what had happened in Hagen earlier in the year.

She felt her twist underneath her over the final double and hesitate slightly as she came to the last oxer. 'Come on girl, we have to jump this', she shouted, as her voice was lost in the wind.

As she galloped through the finish the overreach boot tore completely and was left on the arena floor, just by the timing.

"Another clear for Britain, and inside the time," she heard the announcer say. She'd done it, she'd also jumped double clear for her country. Throwing her arms round her pony's neck she had the broadest grin anyone could remember and started crying with the pure emotion of the moment.

"Well done, well done," said Lorraine as her other team members came to congratulate her.

"Simon you're going to have to jump Danny, up you hop and get him warmed up," said Lorraine.

Two horses later the third German rider was in the ring. This was a vital round and everyone was hoping a fence would fall. The combination was foot perfect until the very last fence, when a bird flew across their path, spooked the pony and took his attention for one vital second. The pole rolled and four faults was added to their tally.

Lorraine was going to find out if her gamble had paid off. She had been hoping Danny wasn't going to have to jump, but he was. He was very experienced, and Simon was known for his ice cool approach, so she had every confidence they could go and jump clear. But she also knew this was a gamble.

At the end of the third round the order at the top

was the same. Germany and Britain on a total of four faults but The Netherlands had moved into third place with some higher scoring rounds from the Swiss, Spanish and French teams.

When called into the ring, Simon looked cool, calm, and confident. Danny looked fit and ready to go and, as they went through the start, Georgie had a good feeling about how this would end. To everyone's delight, Danny jumped a clear, and the cheers that could be heard would stay in Georgie's head for a long time to come.

It all came down to the final German rider, who'd jumped clear the first time. If he jumped clear again, there would be a jump off against the clock, as both teams would end on zero scores.

Riding into the ring, full of confidence, he saluted to the judges. Turning towards where Georgie was standing, she suddenly recognised him. He was the son of the supermarket owner who had tried to buy Allie in Hagen. If the arrogance of his father had rubbed off on his son, Georgie hoped he was going to fail to force a jump off.

Starting off slowly, Georgie could see how carefully he was riding, hoping for the clear round. Every pace was measured, every fence cleared. As he came to the final line, clear, someone in the crowd whistled. Not taking any notice, he kept the same, slow rhythm, and posted the clear the team needed.

"Clear jumping but one and a half time faults," shouted the announcer. You could hear the elation in her voice. His precise German approach had cost his team a jump off for gold. They would have to be satisfied with silver.

Suddenly the collecting ring was a sea of joyful faces, cameras, laughter and cheers. The competition wasn't over, but Great Britain had won. People were flocking to congratulate the team and Lorraine and Gerald were hugging each other while trying to keep their team safe.

Some 40 minutes later, with the results confirmed, winning rugs on the ponies and the team trotting into the ring, Georgie was pinching herself and would find bruises on her arms the next day.

She'd won. The whole year she had focused on this one championship. And she was standing on the podium, having a gold medal placed around her neck and holding a bouquet of flowers in her hands. Lizzie was holding Allie who was enjoying the sashes and rosettes put around her neck and on to her bridle, while another official was walking along the line with a basket of carrots and apples.

As God Save the Queen rang out, and the union flag was raised, she'd never felt so proud. Unable to stop the tears from running down her cheeks, she whispered her thanks to the special pony that had brought her so far. They were now the perfect partnership.

This is what she'd wanted for so long. This was her

leap into the world she loved.

There was still one more year in ponies to come, one more chance in 12 months' time to win double gold – the individual and the team.

But that was in the future. This was now.

30 - 00 -01

GI S4

5C S 4

07 8S0
6 2 4 8 17